Beak & Ally

Unlikely Friends

Norm Feuti

HARPER alley

An Imprint of HarperCollinsPublishers

To all my friends, likely or otherwise.

One

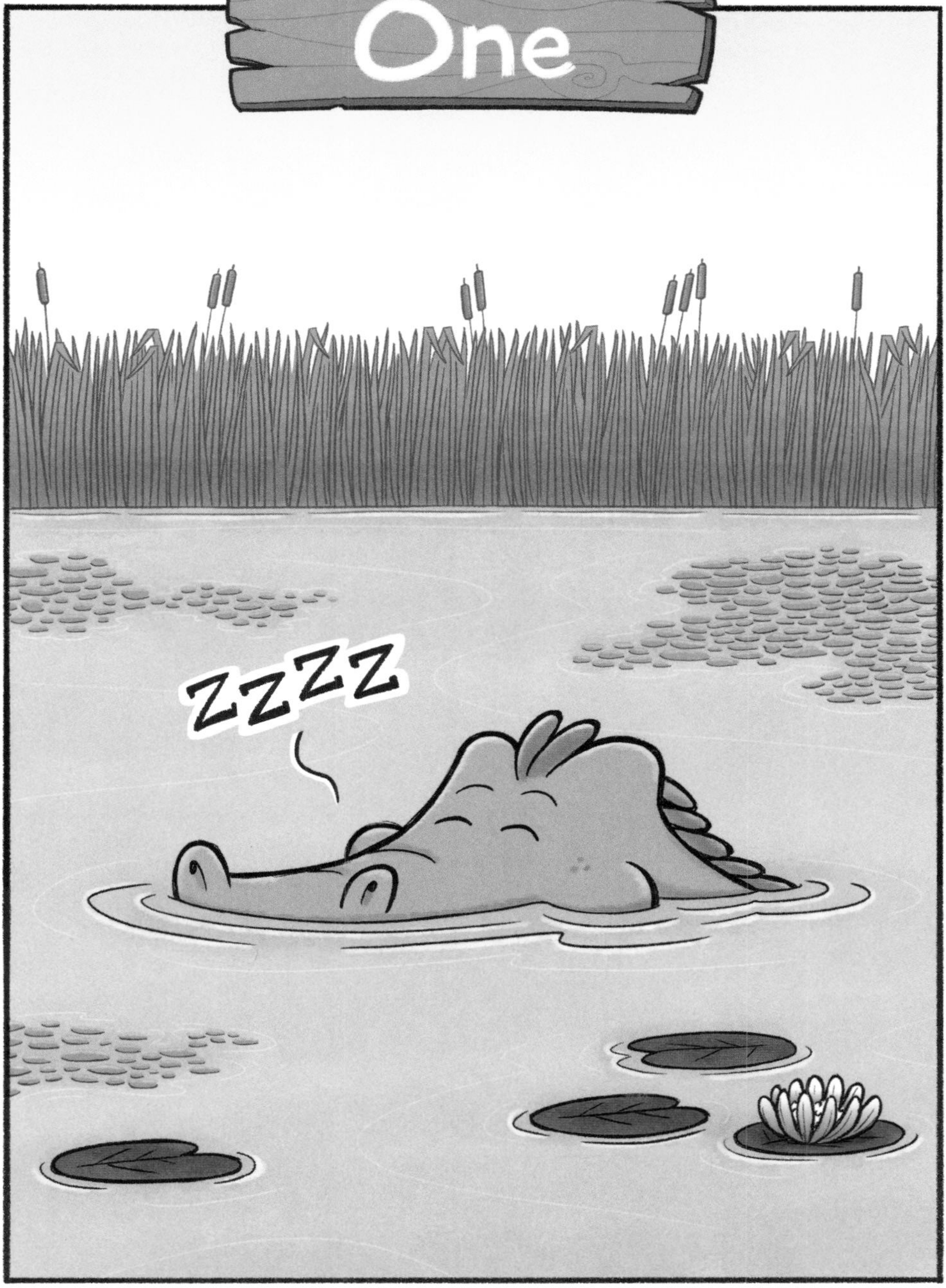
ZZZZ

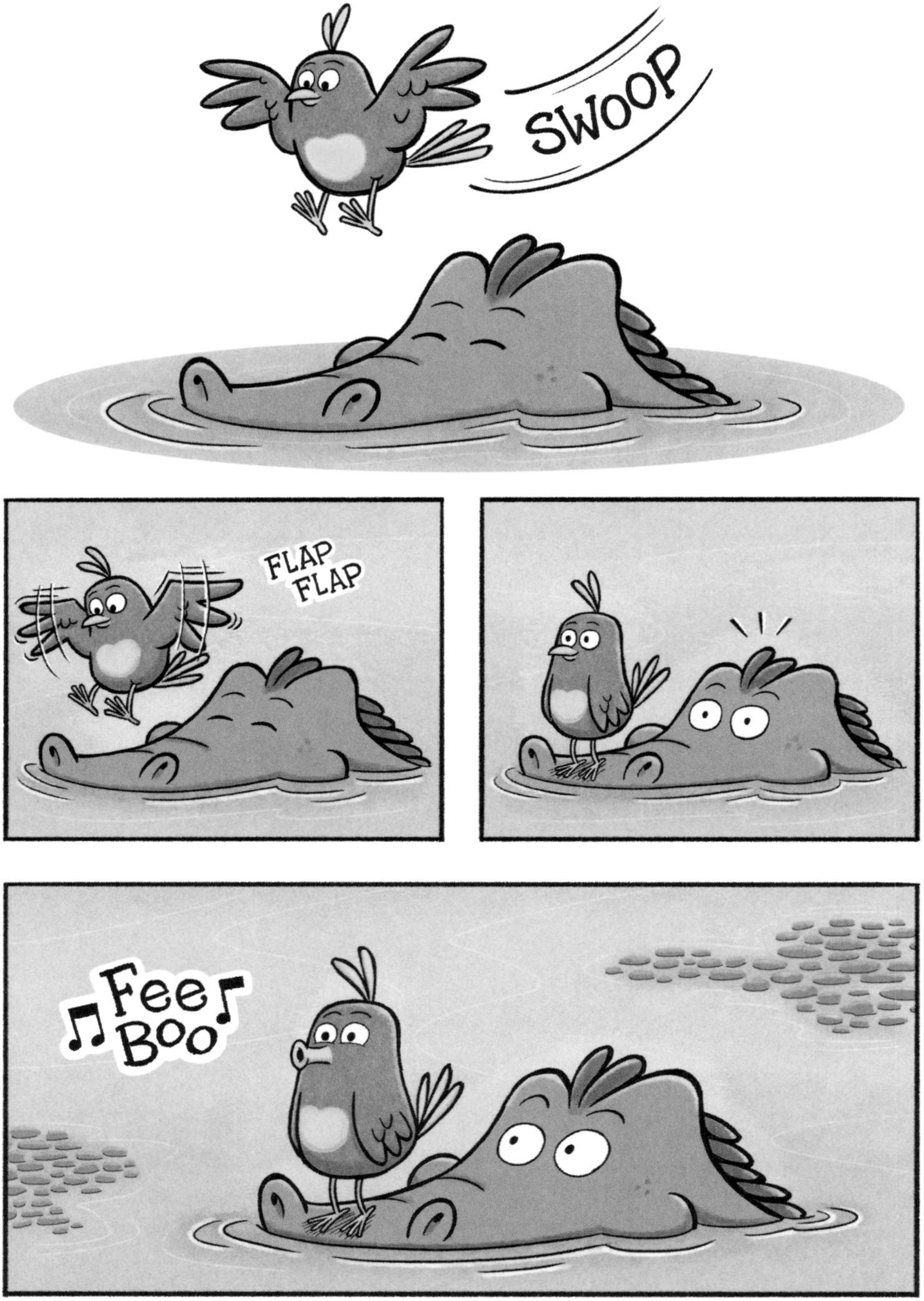
SWOOP
FLAP
FLAP
Fee
Boo

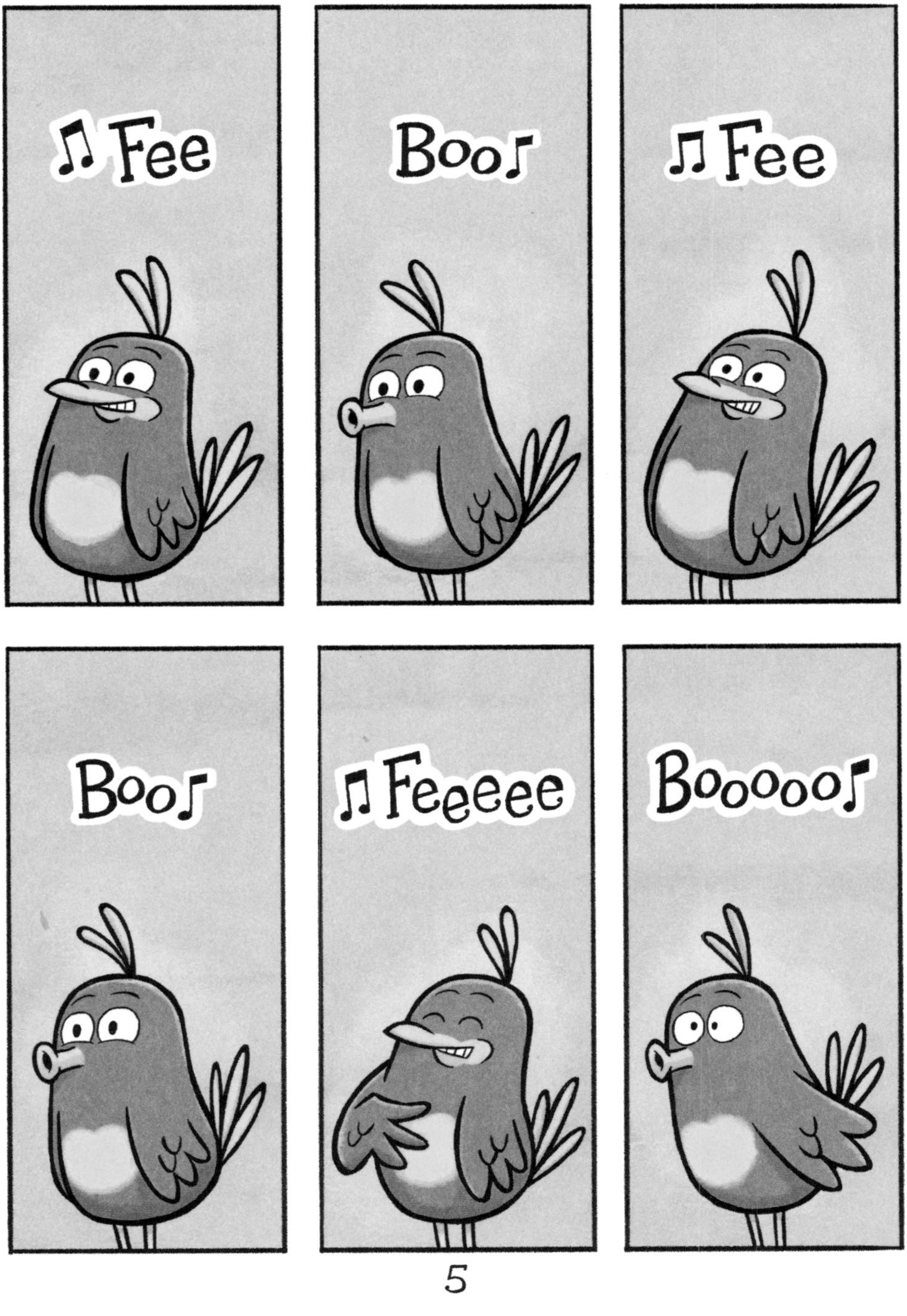
♫ Fee
Boo♪
♫ Fee
Boo♪
♫ Feeeee
Booooo♪

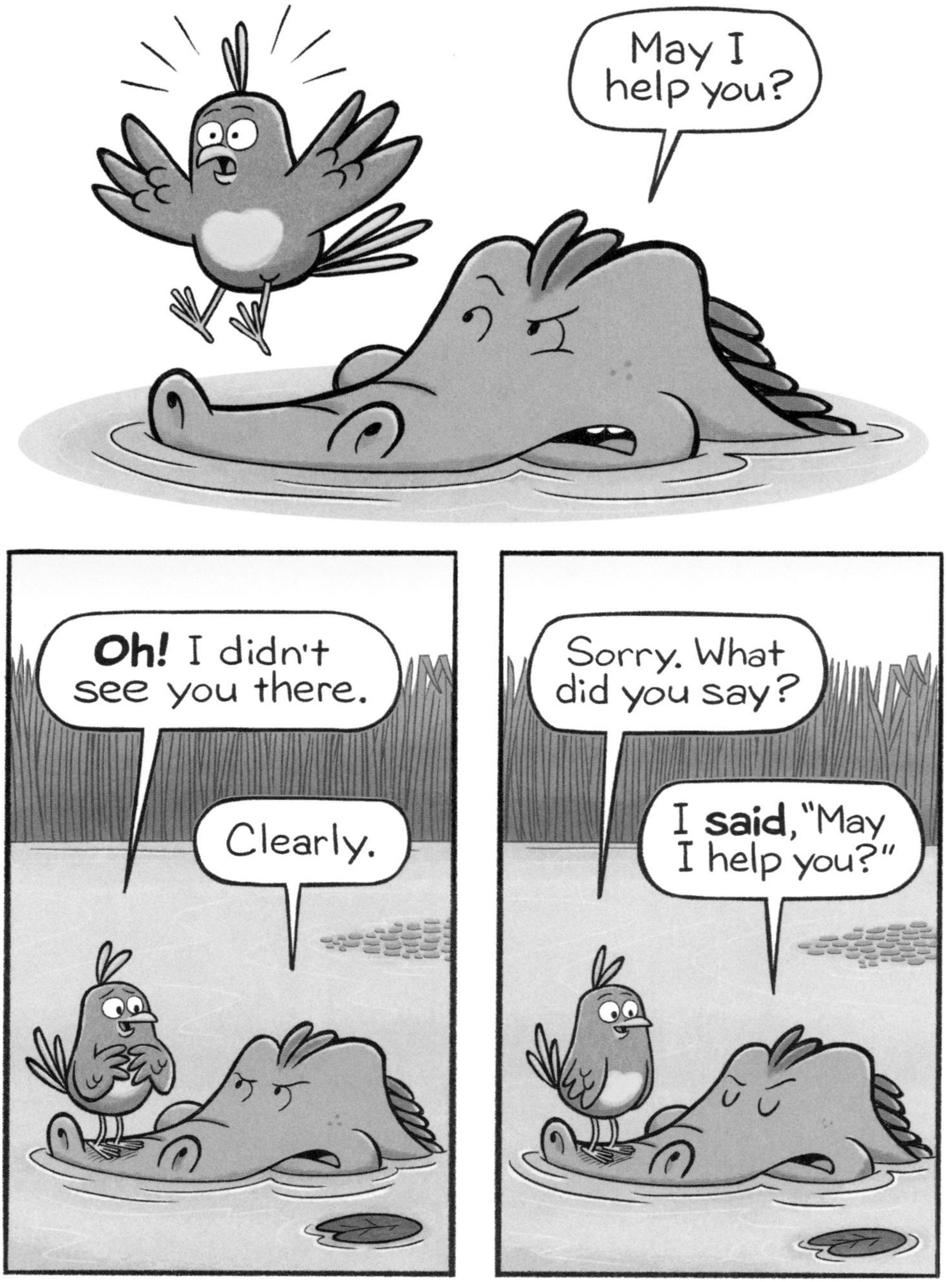
May I help you?
Oh! I didn't see you there.
Clearly.
Sorry. What did you say?
I **said**, "May I help you?"

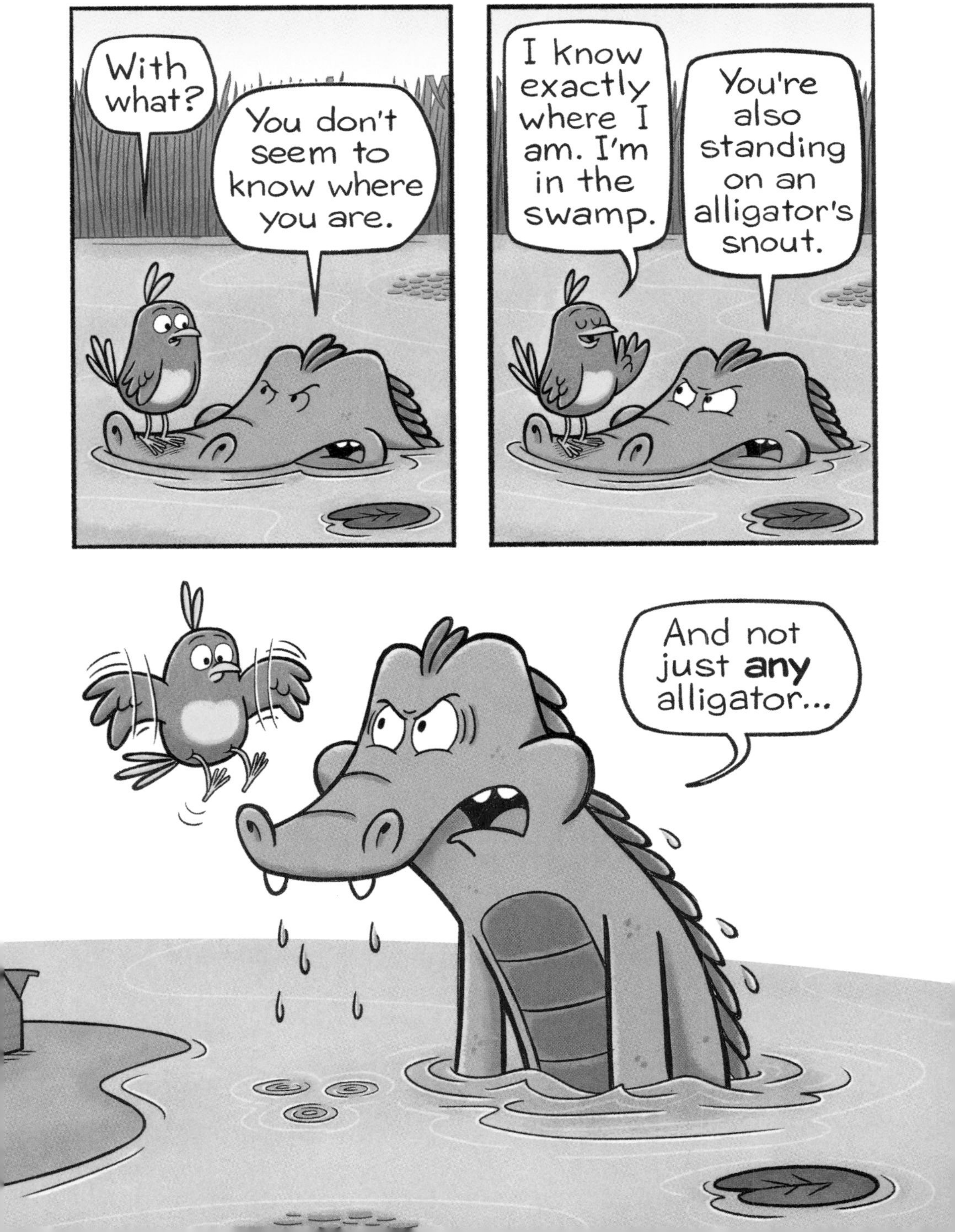
With what?
You don't seem to know where you are.
I know exactly where I am. I'm in the swamp.
You're also standing on an alligator's snout.
And not just **any** alligator...

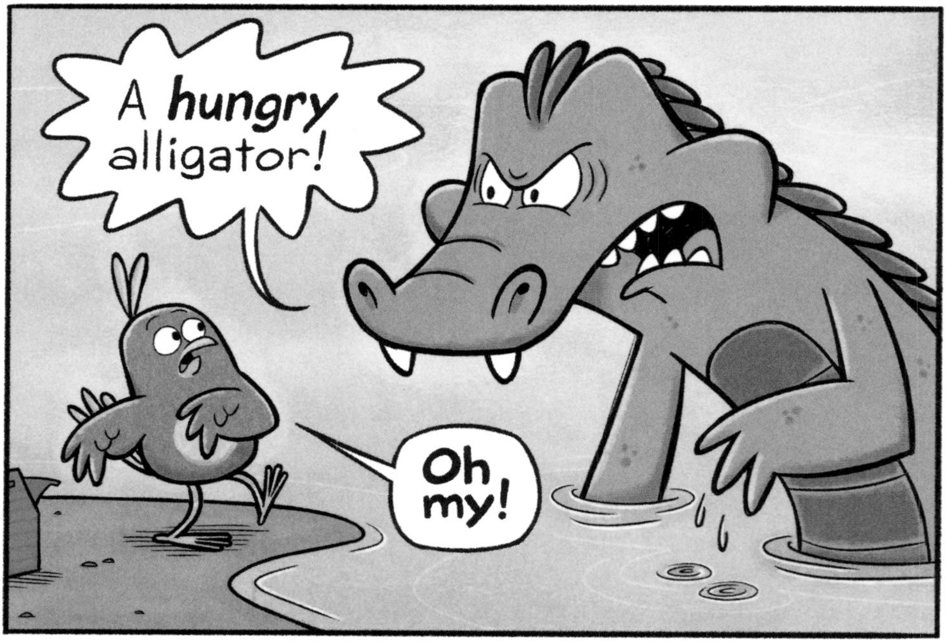
A **hungry** alligator!
Oh my!

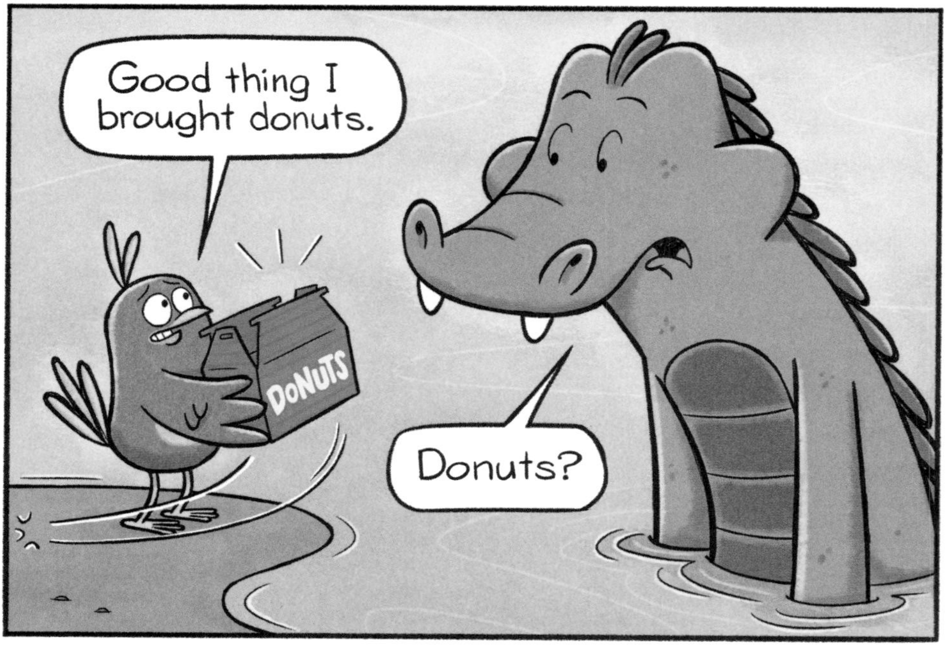
Good thing I brought donuts.
DONUTS
Donuts?

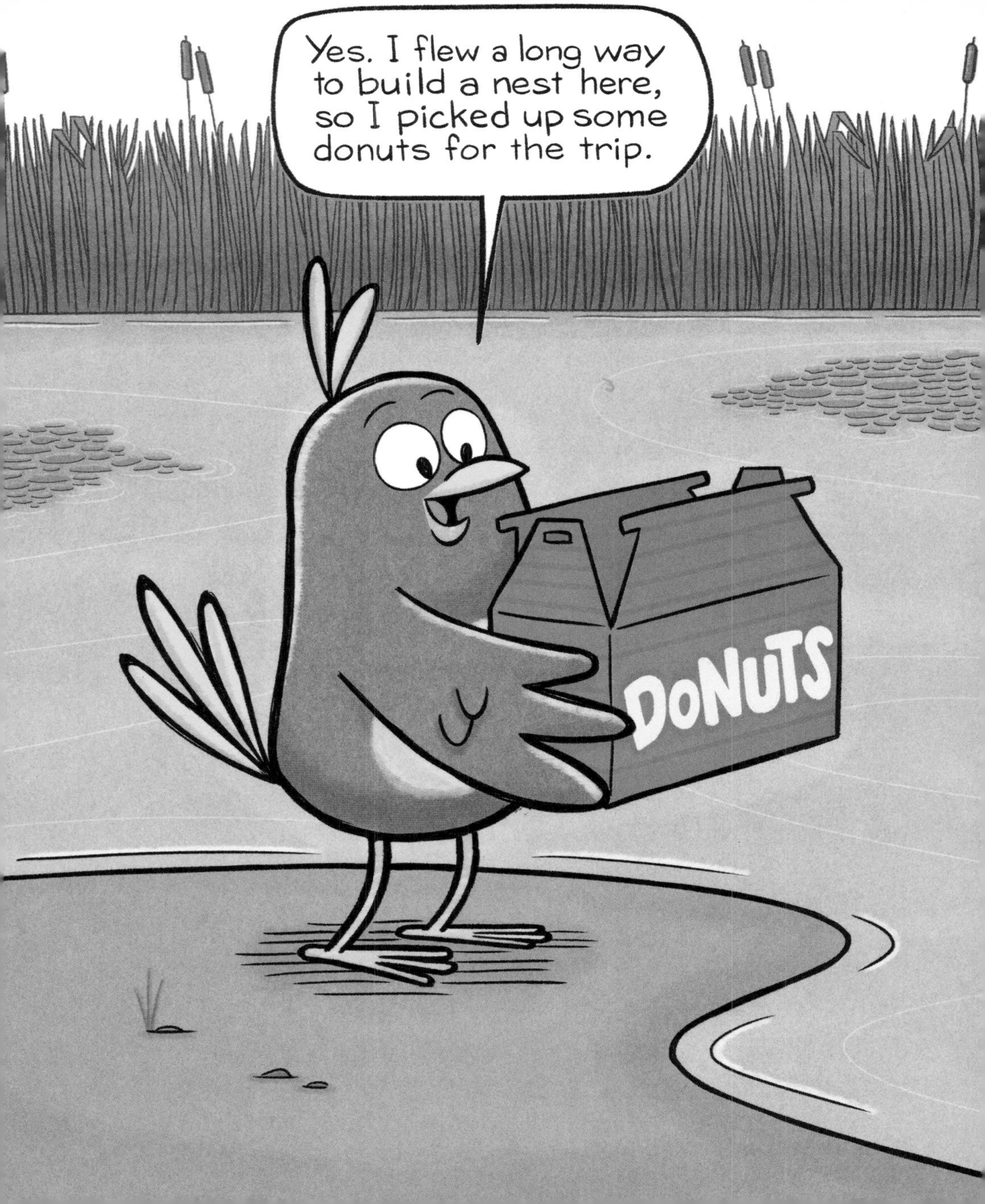
Yes. I flew a long way to build a nest here, so I picked up some donuts for the trip.
DONUTS

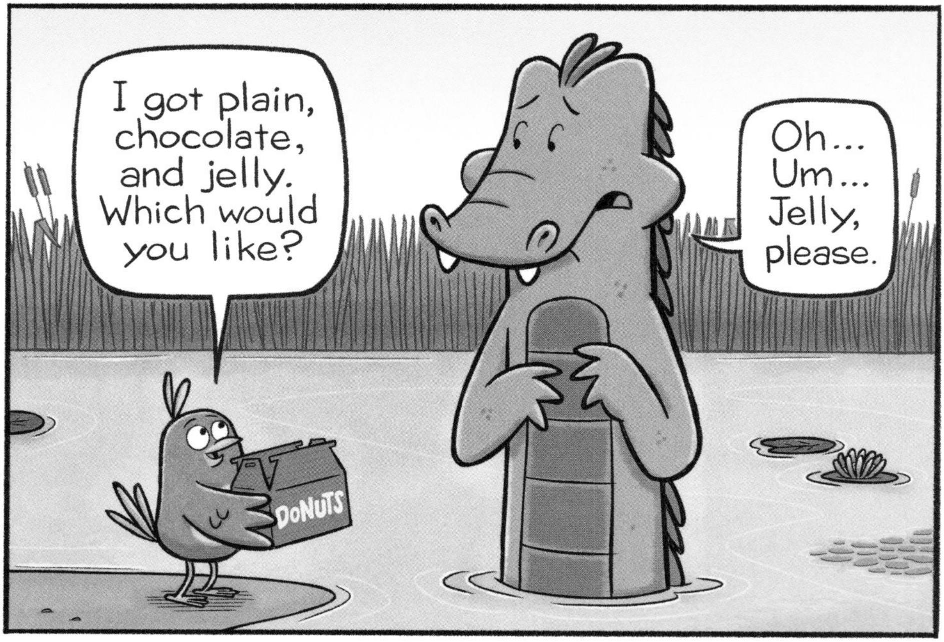
I got plain, chocolate, and jelly. Which would you like?
Oh... Um... Jelly, please.
DONUTS

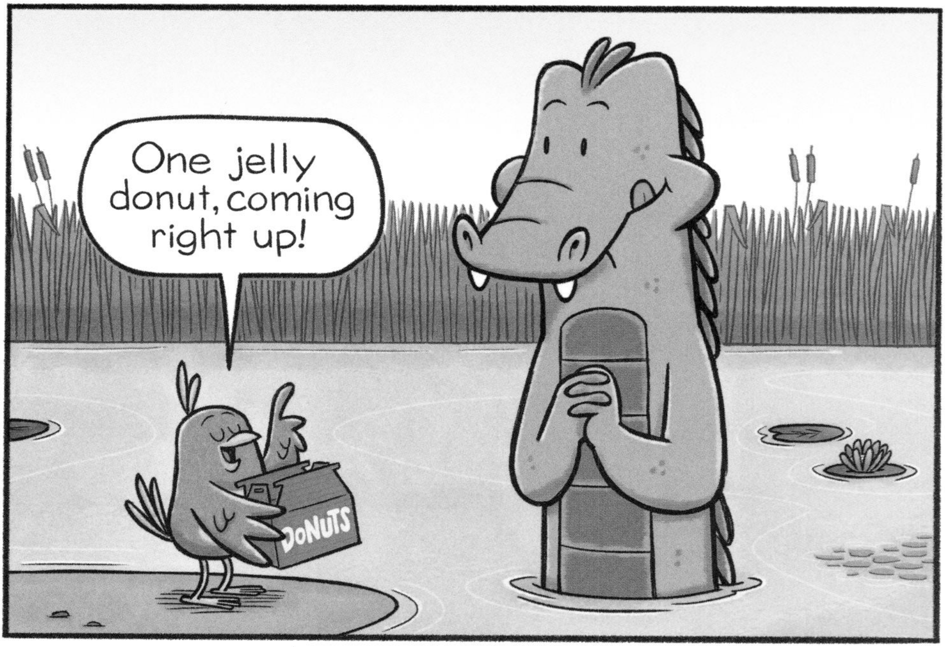
One jelly donut, coming right up!
DONUTS

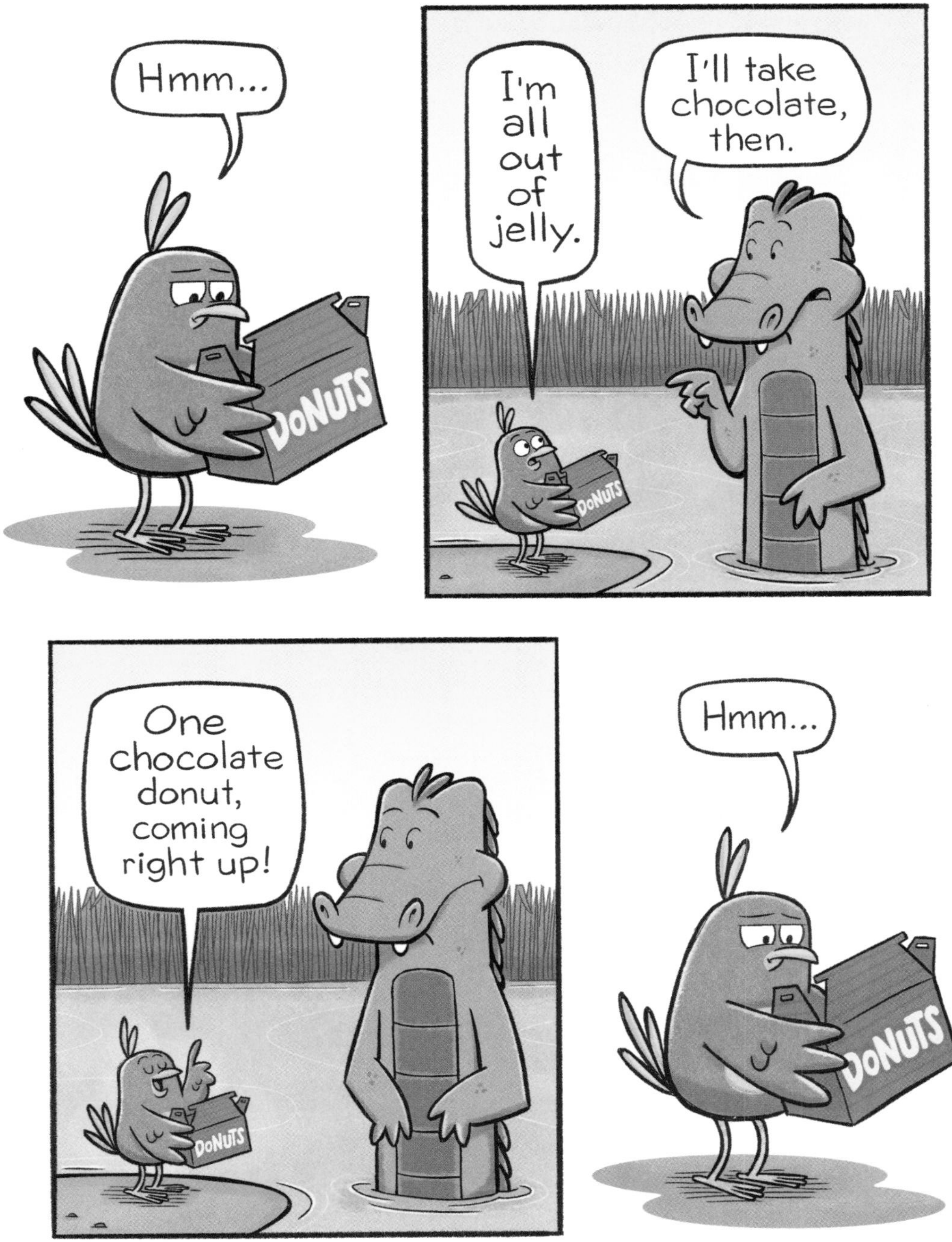
Hmm...
I'm all out of jelly.
I'll take chocolate, then.
One chocolate donut, coming right up!
Hmm...
DONUTS

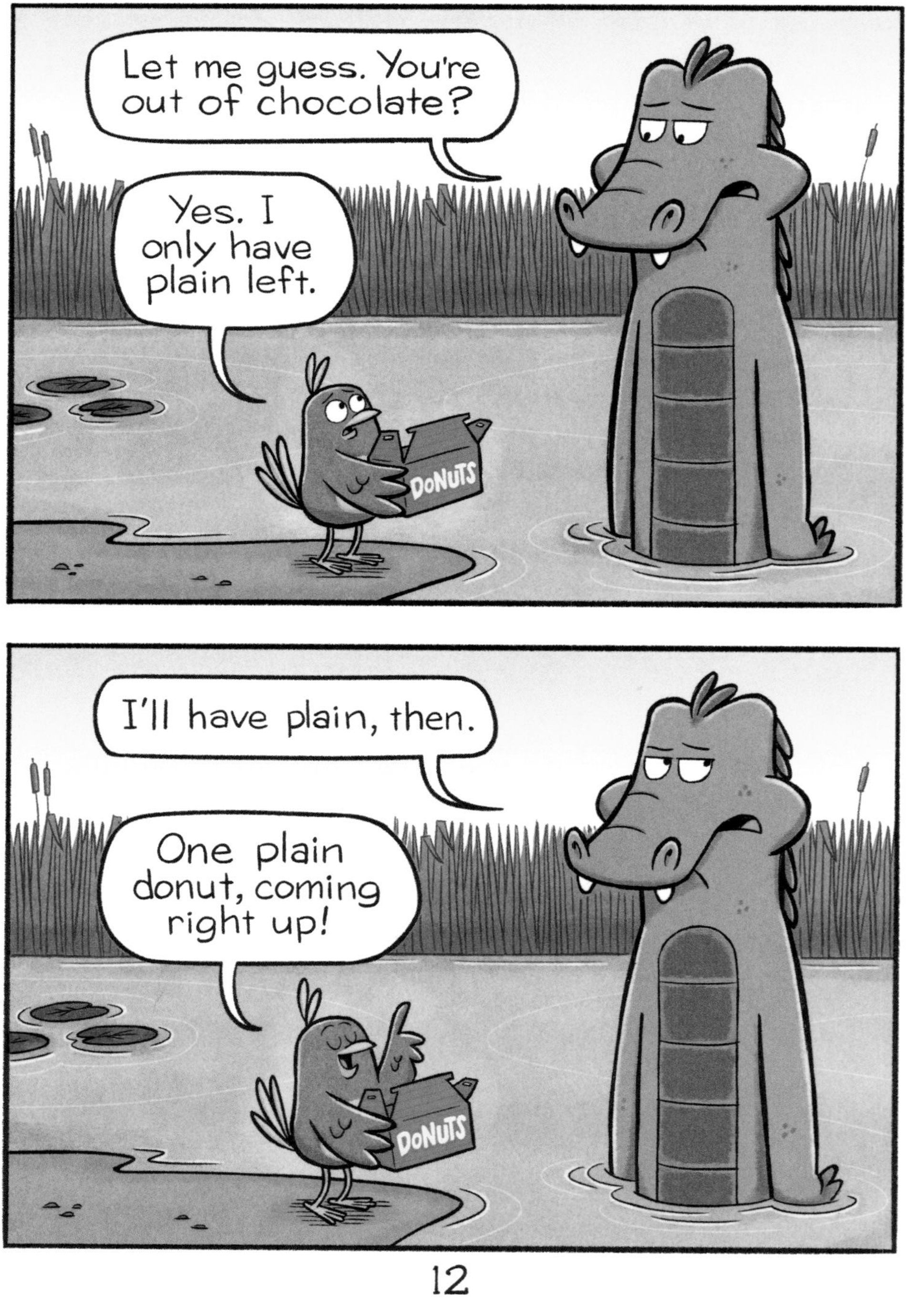
Let me guess. You're out of chocolate?
Yes. I only have plain left.
DONUTS
I'll have plain, then.
One plain donut, coming right up!
DONUTS

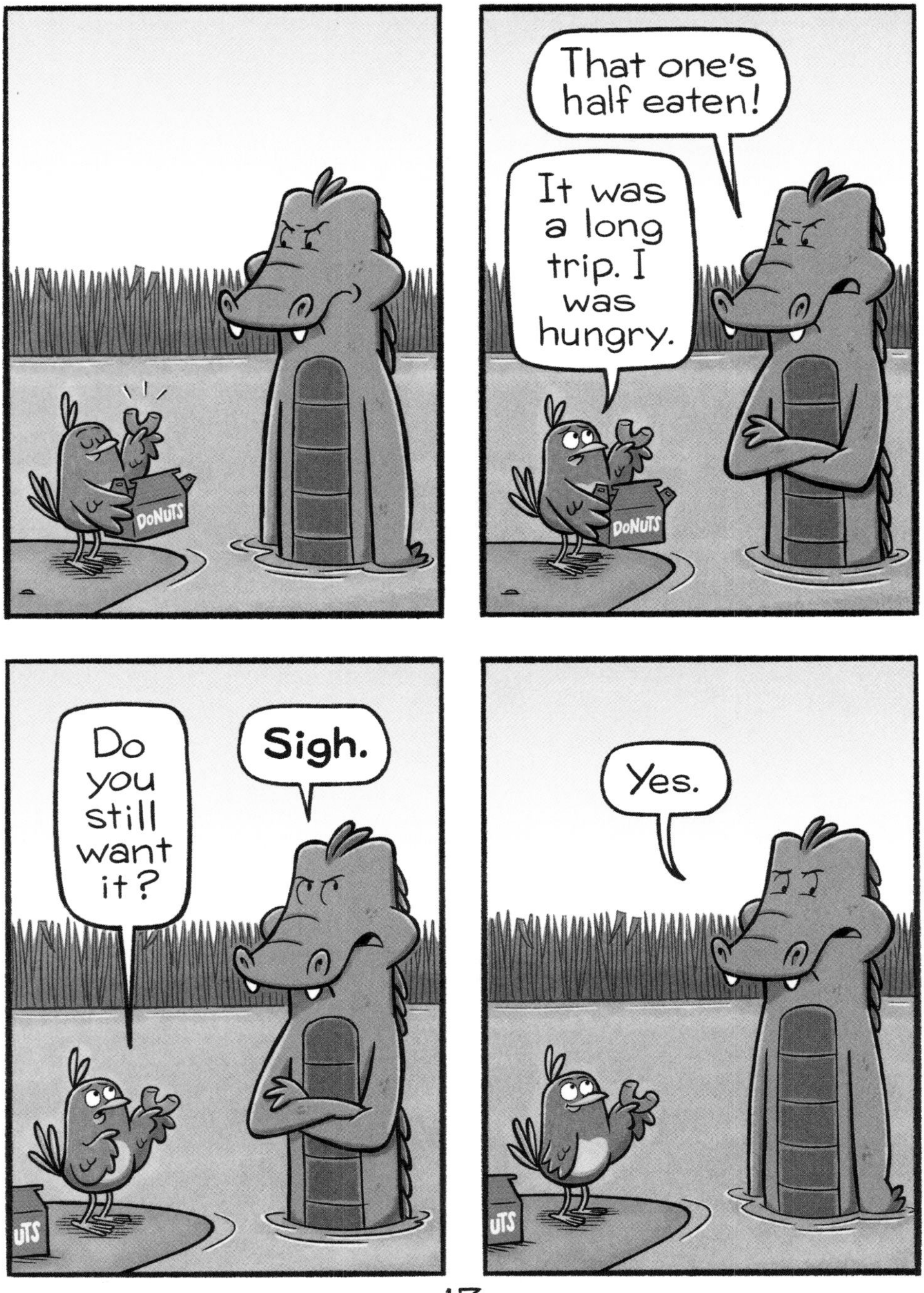
DONUTS
That one's half eaten!
It was a long trip. I was hungry.
DONUTS
Do you still want it?
Sigh.
Yes.

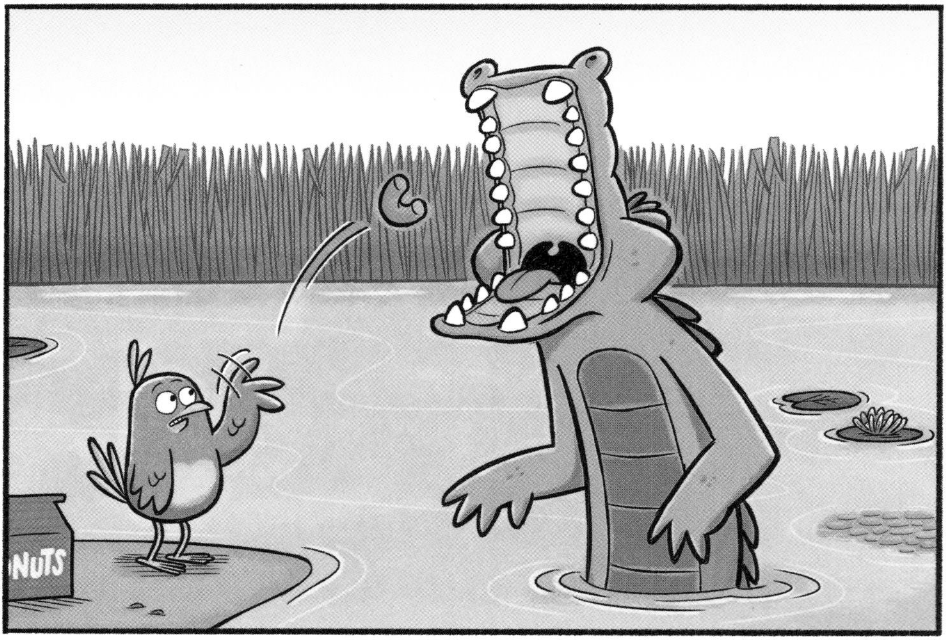
NUTS

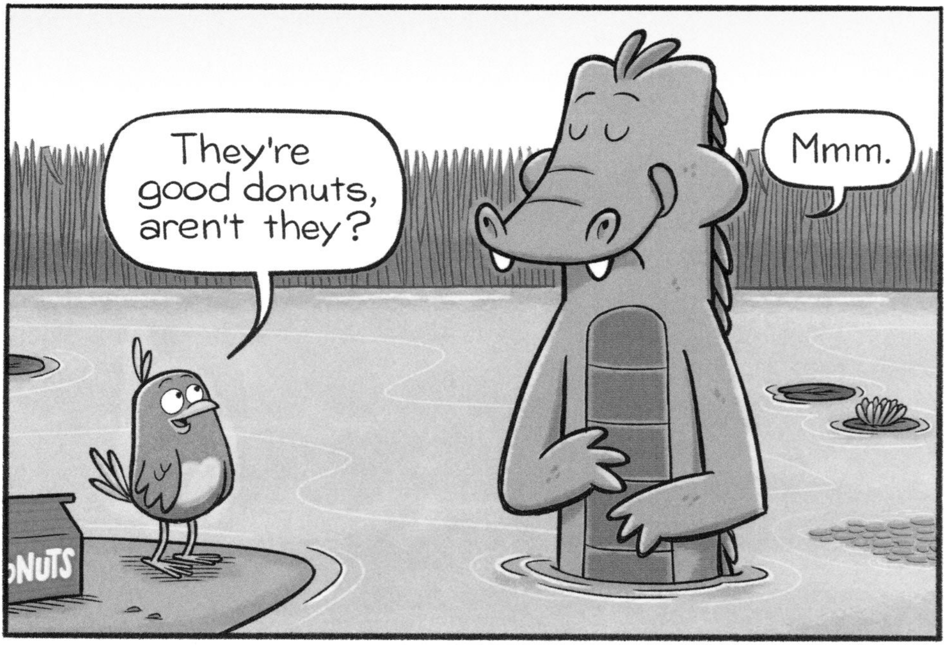
They're good donuts, aren't they?
Mmm.
NUTS

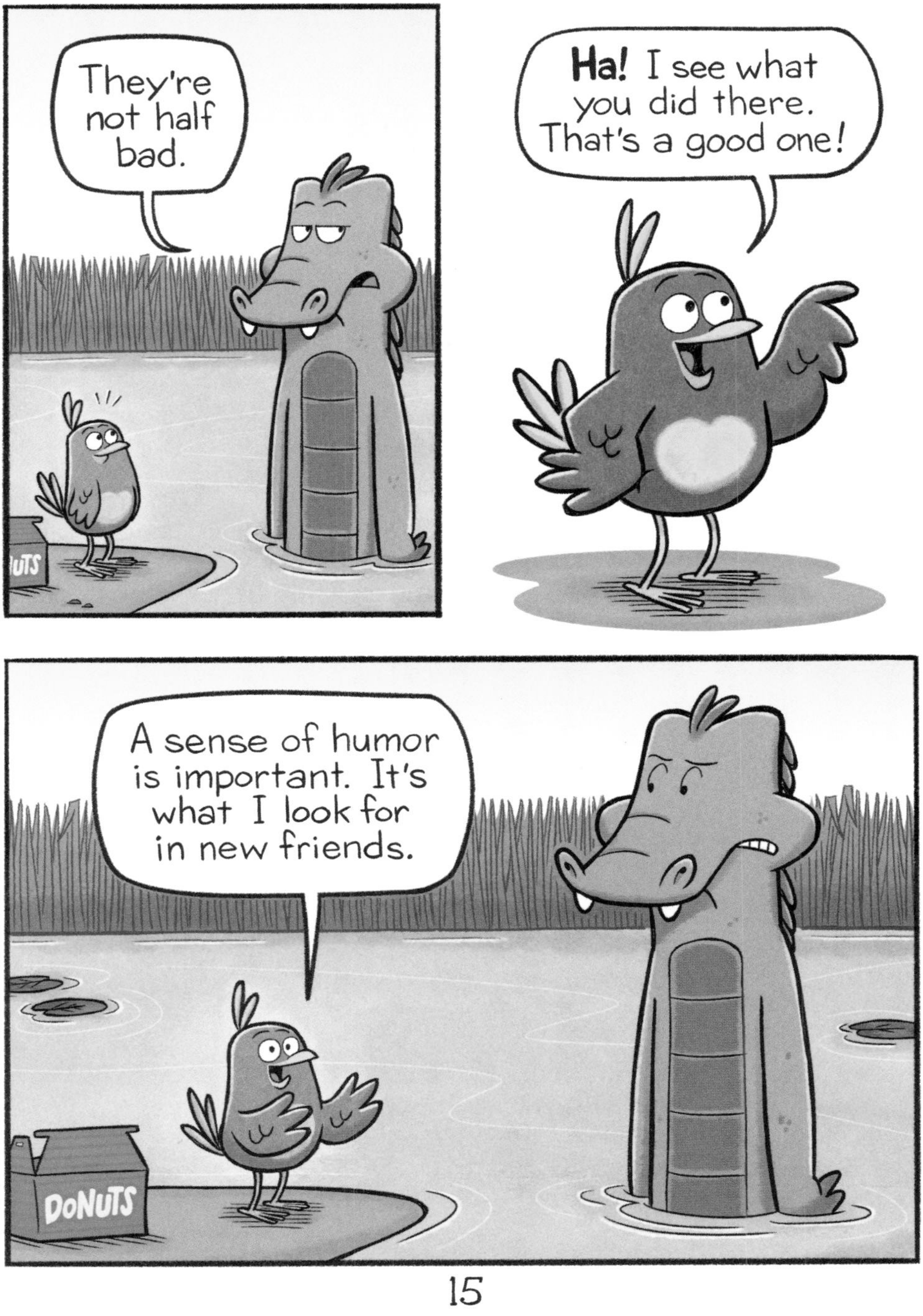
They're not half bad.
Ha! I see what you did there. That's a good one!
UTS
A sense of humor is important. It's what I look for in new friends.
DONUTS

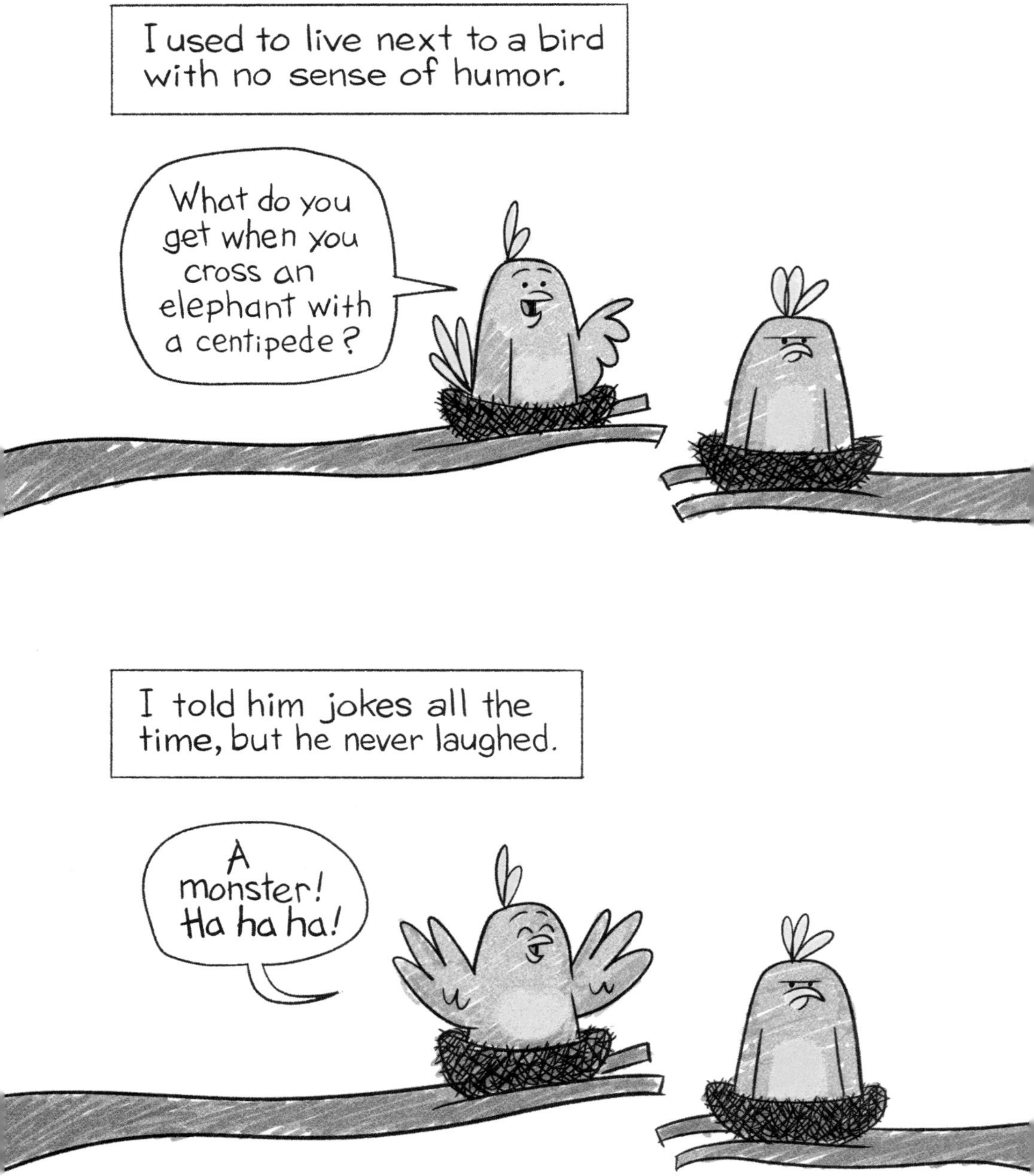
I used to live next to a bird with no sense of humor.
What do you get when you cross an elephant with a centipede?
I told him jokes all the time, but he never laughed.
A monster! Ha ha ha!

I didn't give up, though. I kept trying, day after day.

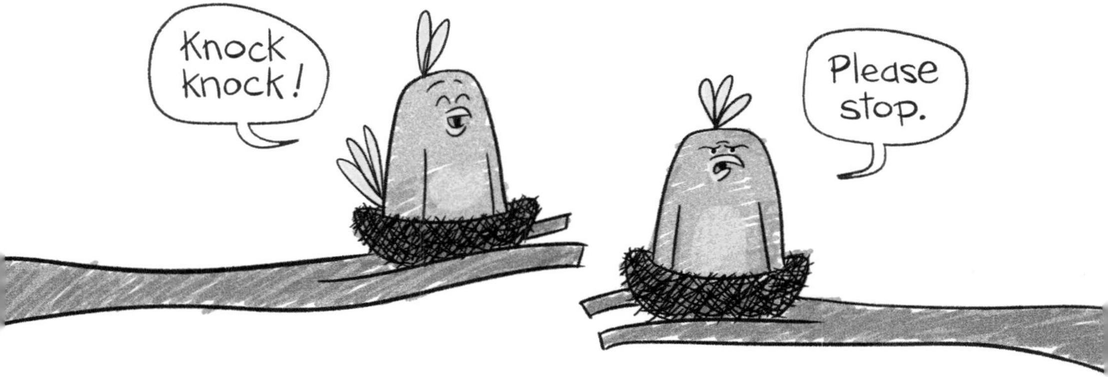
Knock knock!
Please stop.

Until he moved away suddenly.

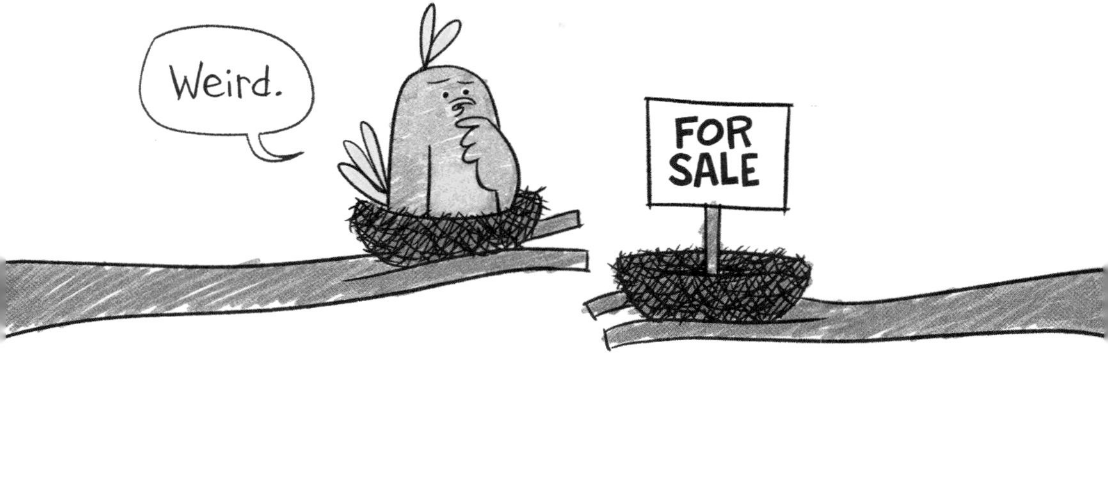
Weird.
FOR SALE

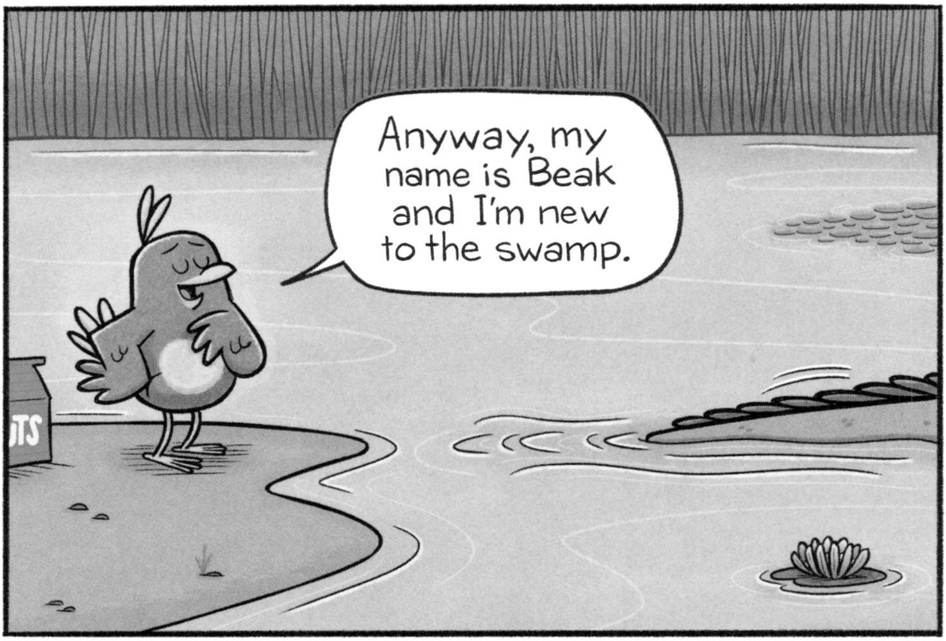
Anyway, my name is Beak and I'm new to the swamp.
UTS

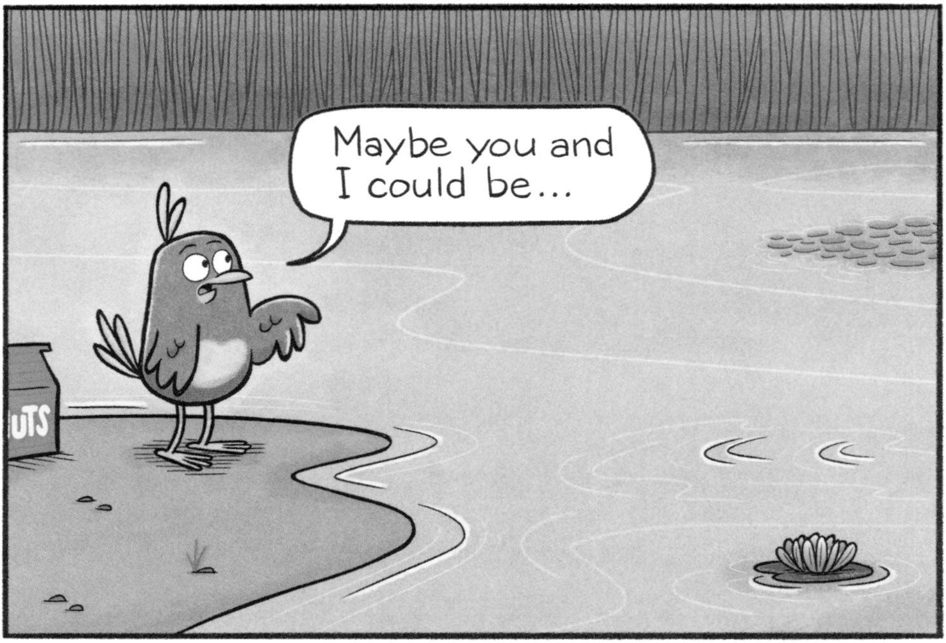
Maybe you and I could be...
UTS

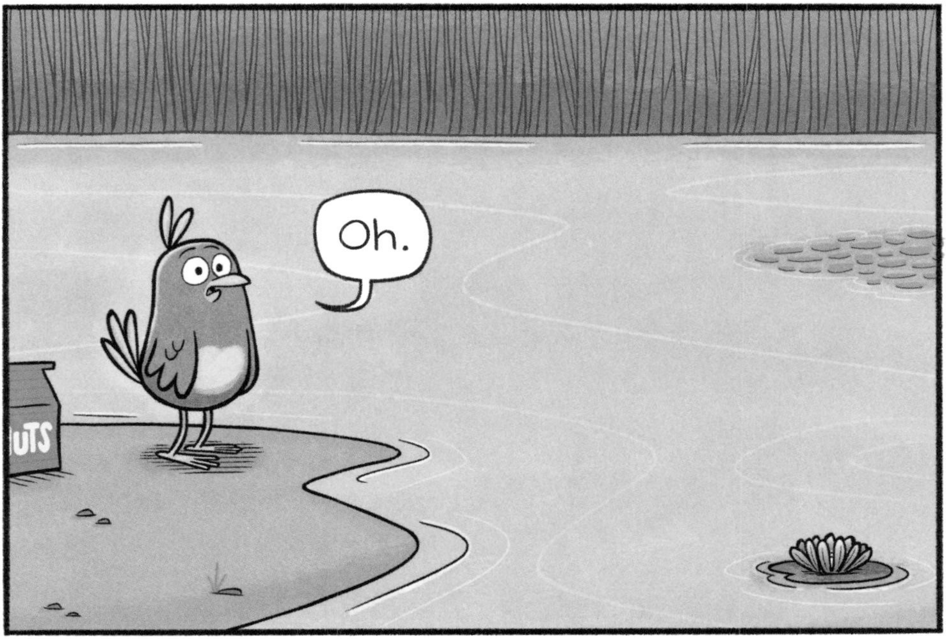
Oh.

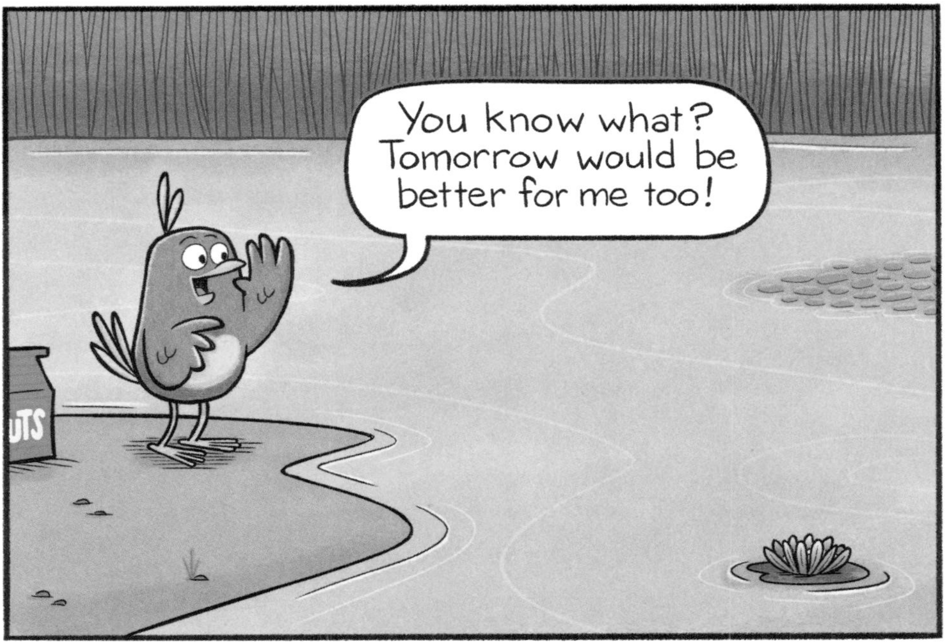
You know what? Tomorrow would be better for me too!

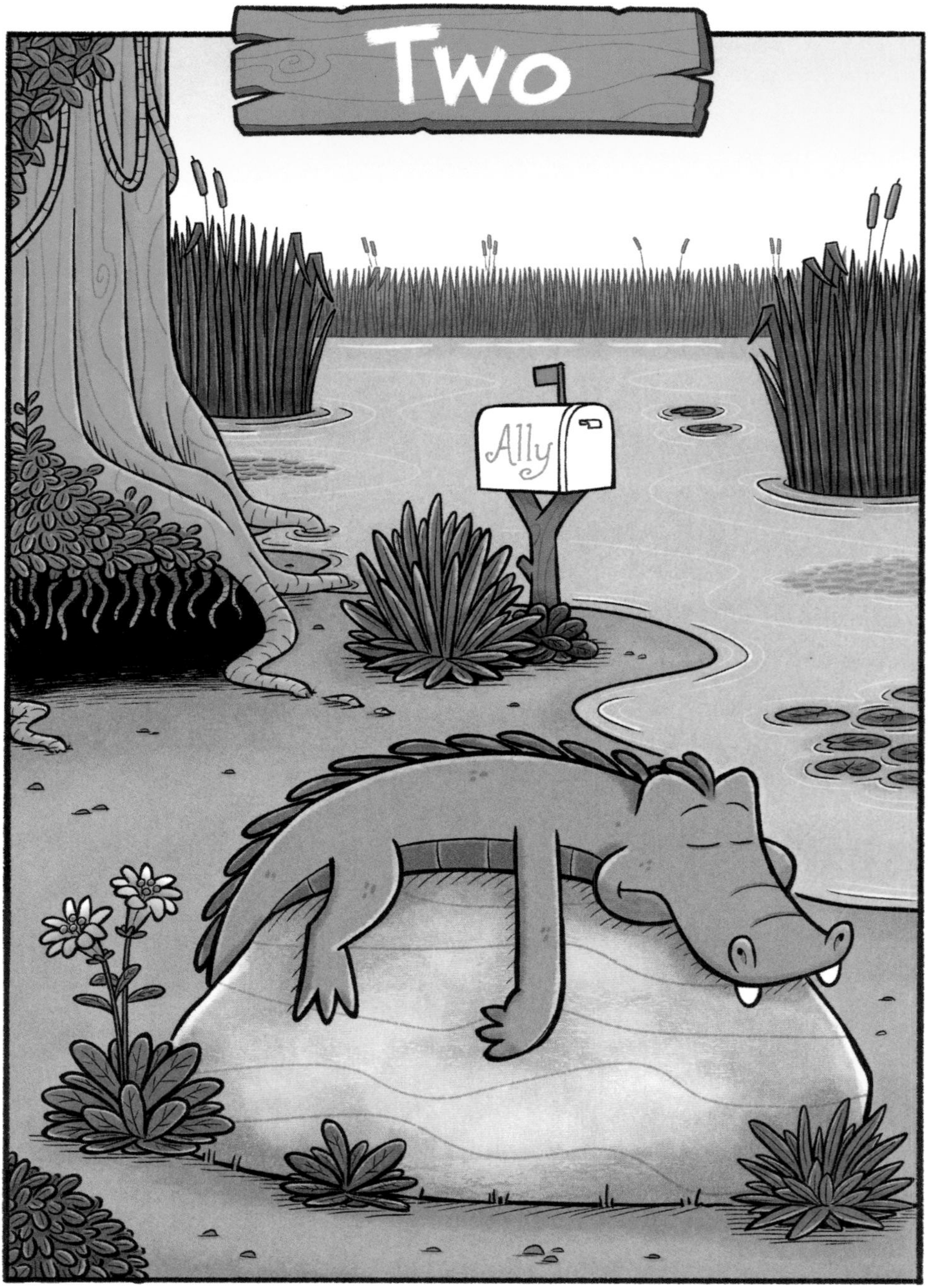
Two
Ally

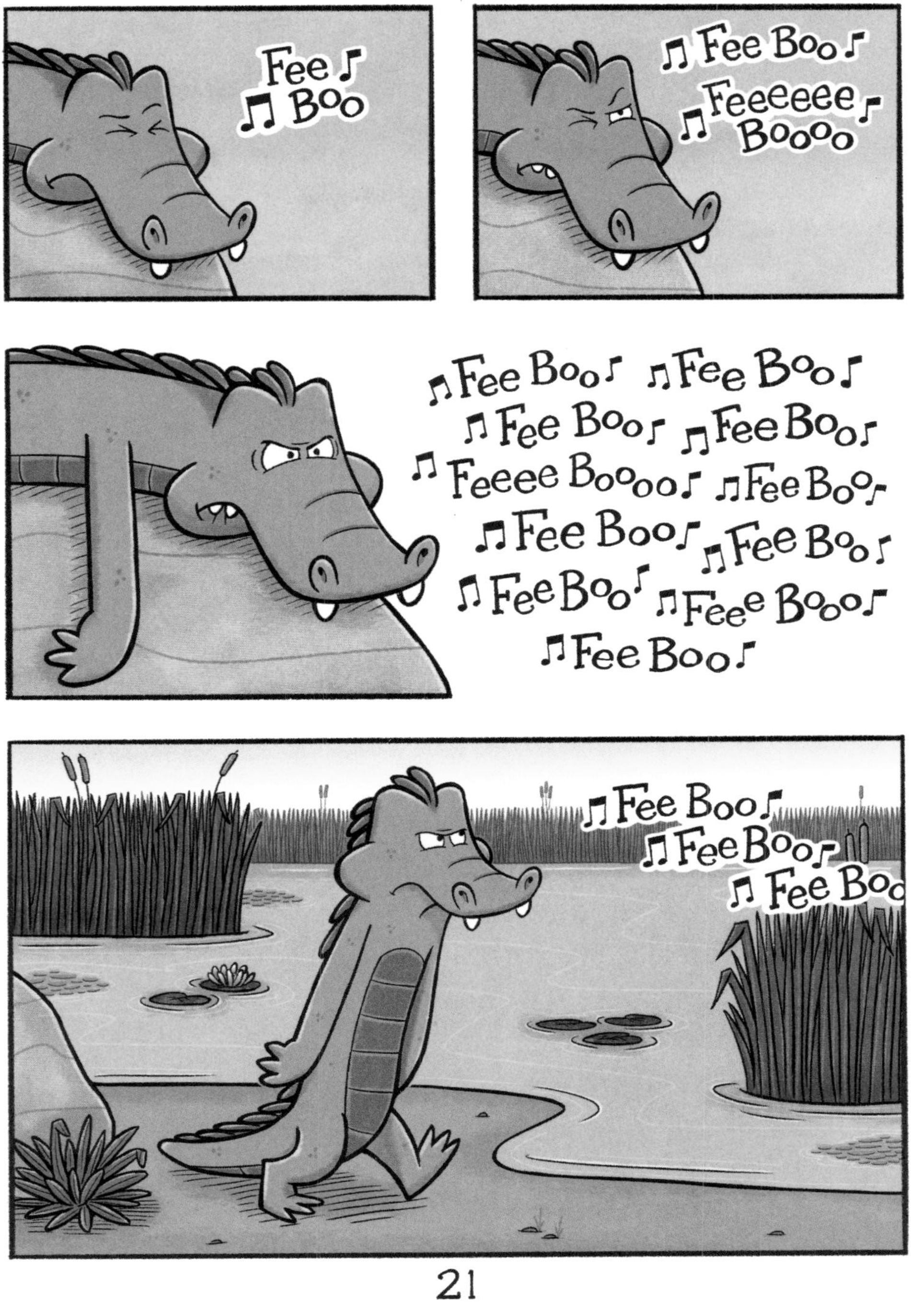
Fee ♪
♫ Boo
♫ Fee Boo ♪
♫ Feeeeee ♪
Boooo
♫ Fee Boo ♪ ♫ Fee Boo ♪
♫ Fee Boo ♪ ♫ Fee Boo ♪
♫ Feeee Booooo ♪ ♫ Fee Boo ♪
♫ Fee Boo ♪ ♫ Fee Boo ♪
♫ Fee Boo ♪ ♫ Feee Booo ♪
♫ Fee Boo ♪
♫ Fee Boo ♪
♫ Fee Boo ♪
♫ Fee Bo

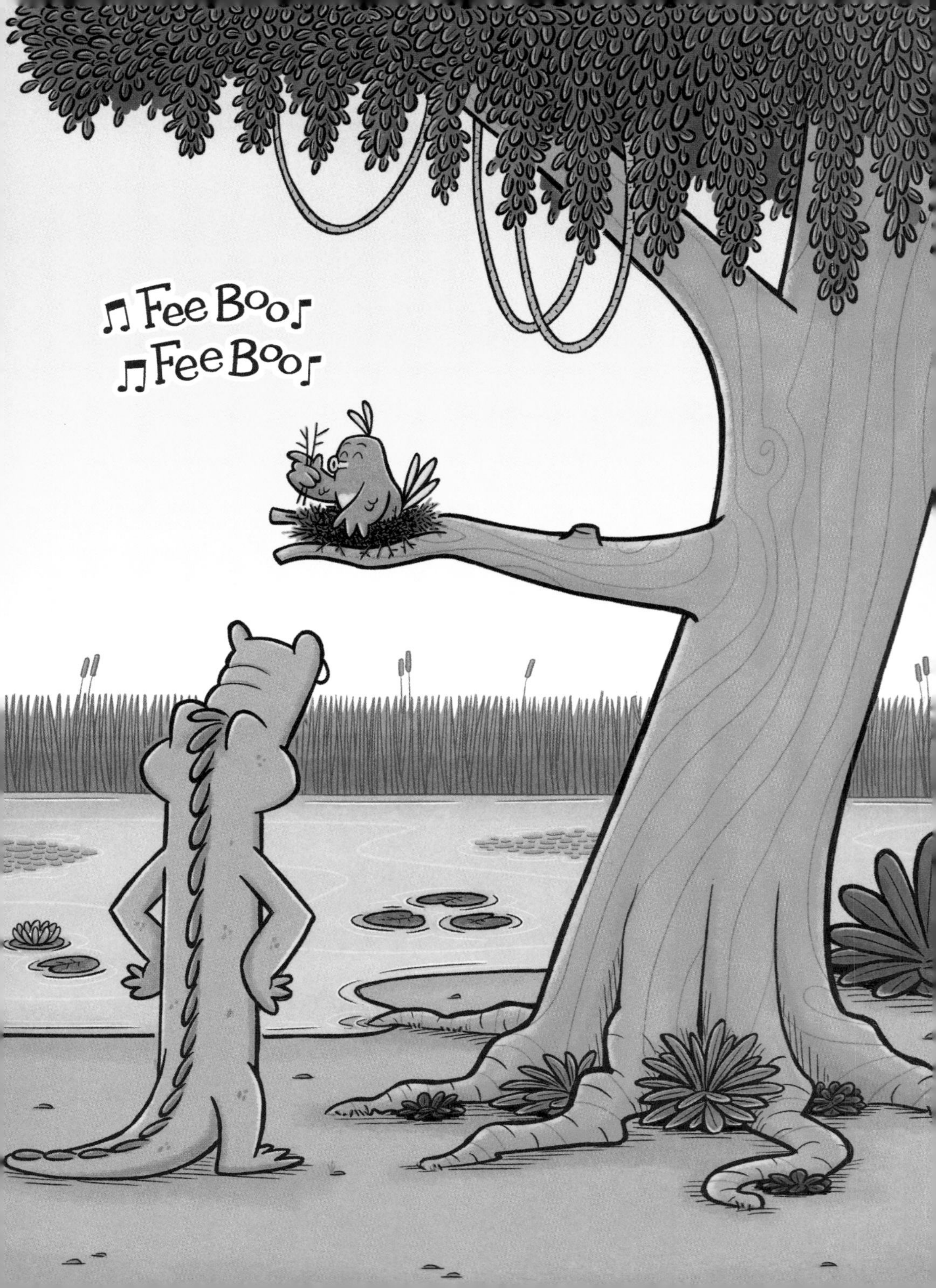
Fee Boo
Fee Boo

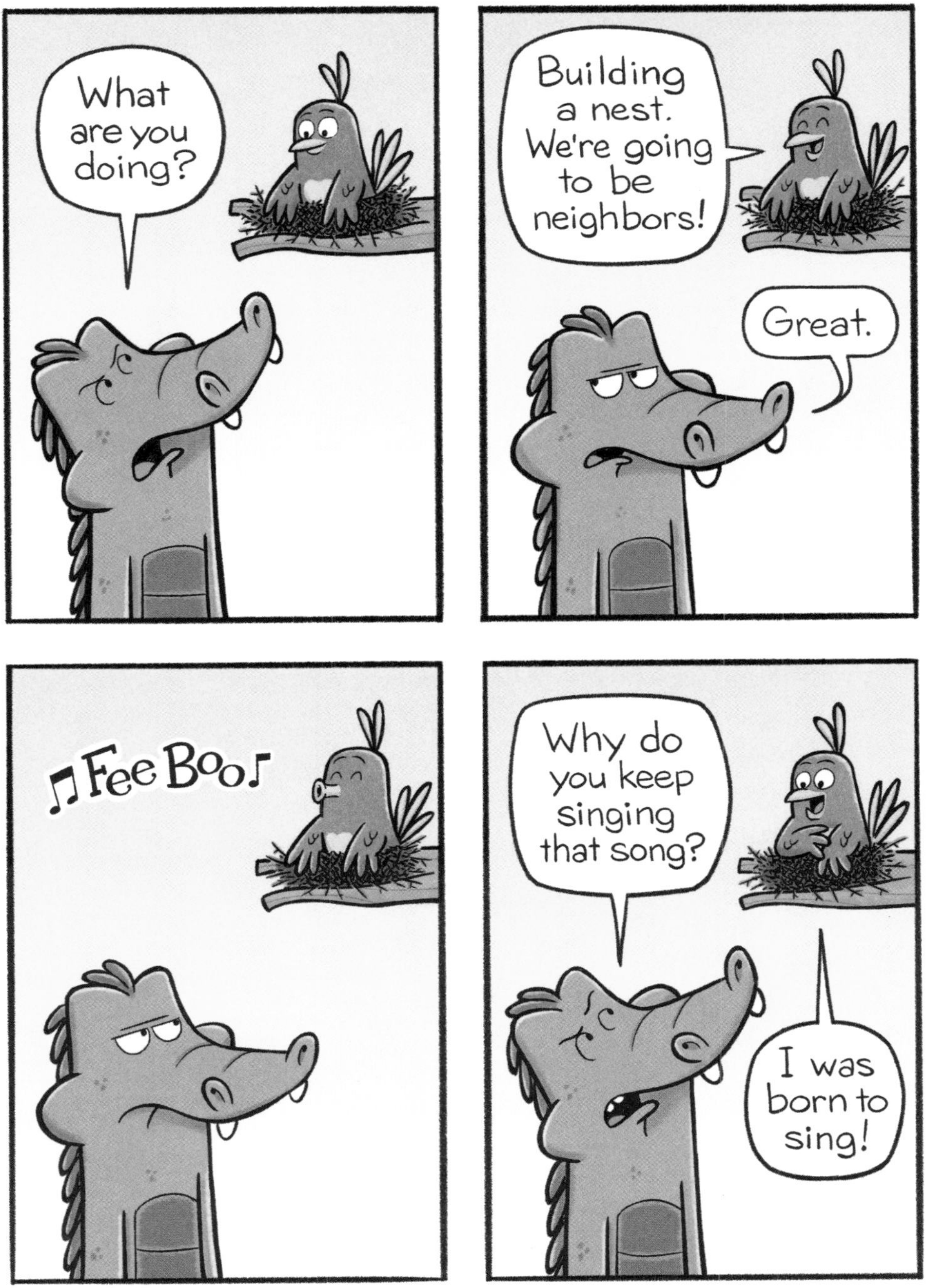
What are you doing?
Building a nest. We're going to be neighbors!
Great.
♫ Fee Boo ♪
Why do you keep singing that song?
I was born to sing!

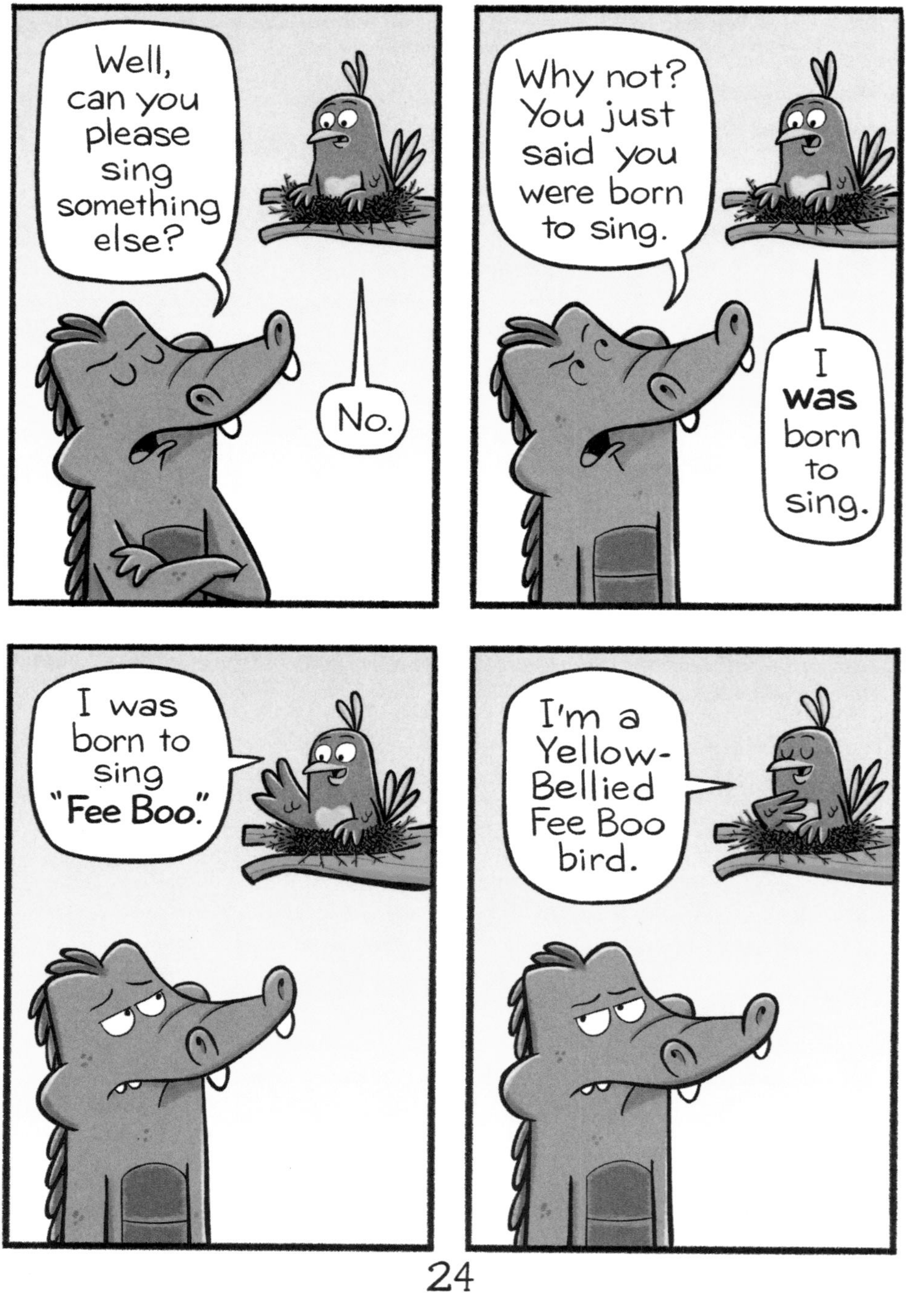
Well, can you please sing something else?
No.
Why not? You just said you were born to sing.
I **was** born to sing.
I was born to sing "**Fee Boo**."
I'm a Yellow-Bellied Fee Boo bird.

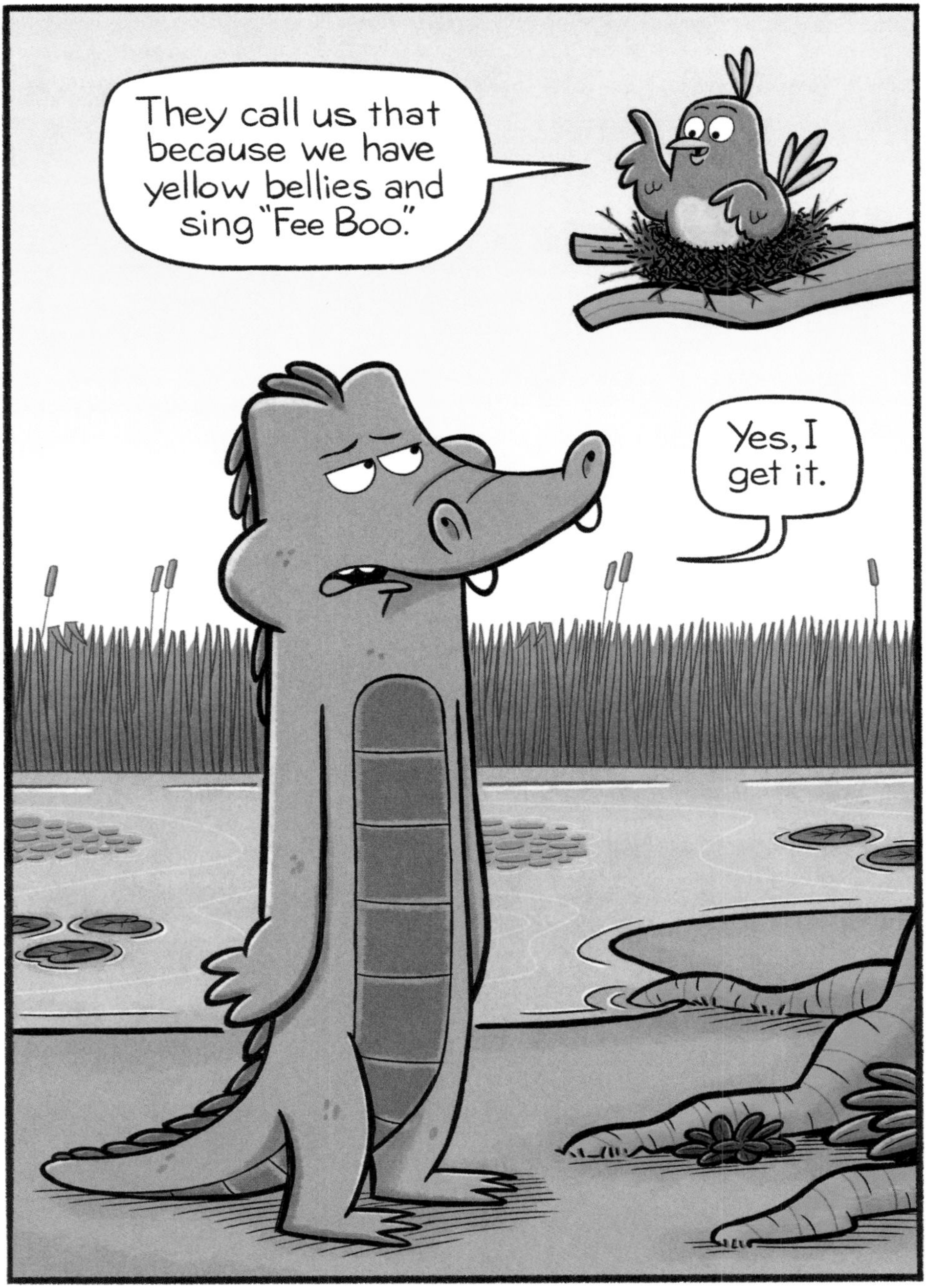
They call us that because we have yellow bellies and sing "Fee Boo."
Yes, I get it.

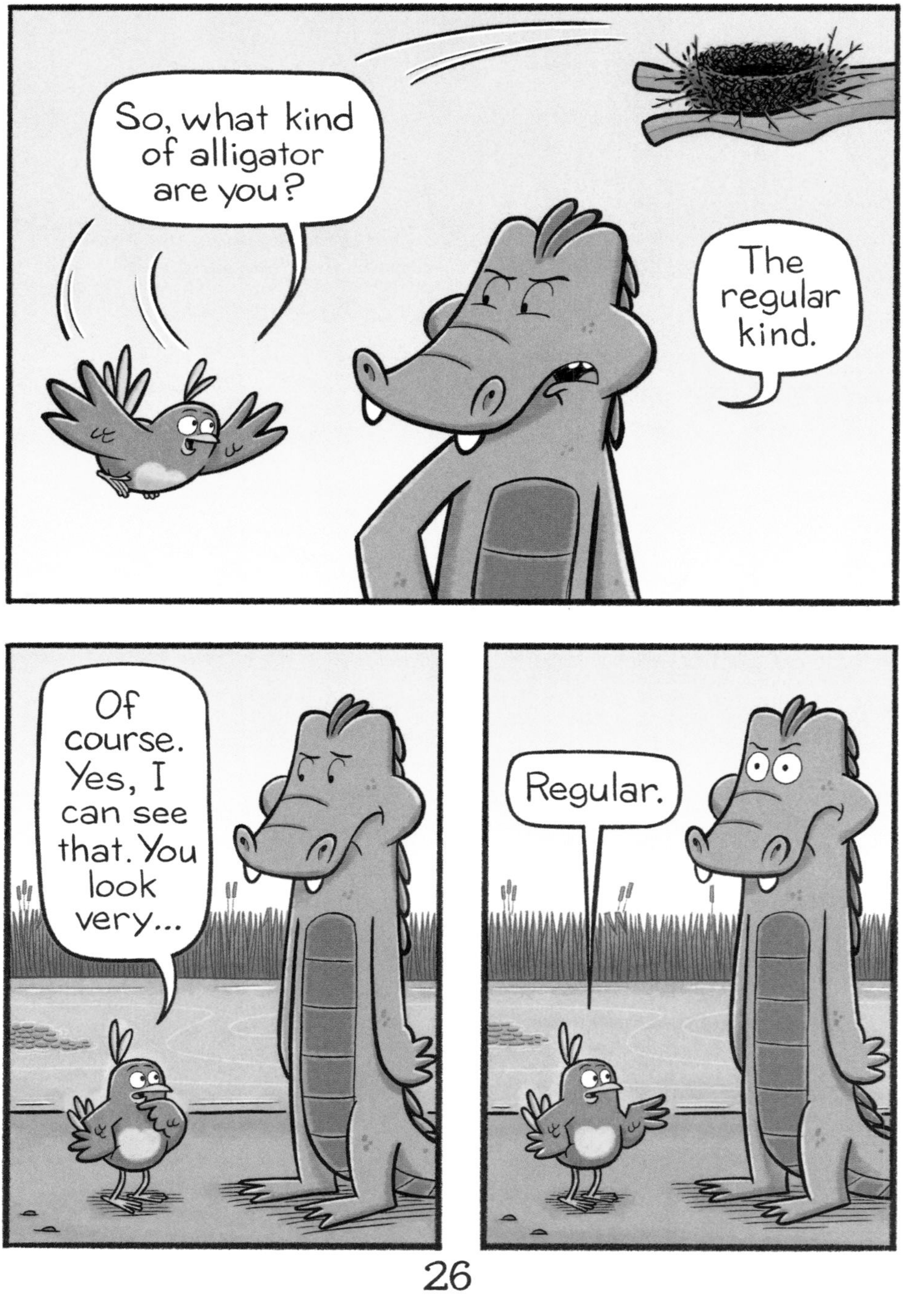
So, what kind of alligator are you?
The regular kind.
Of course. Yes, I can see that. You look very...
Regular.

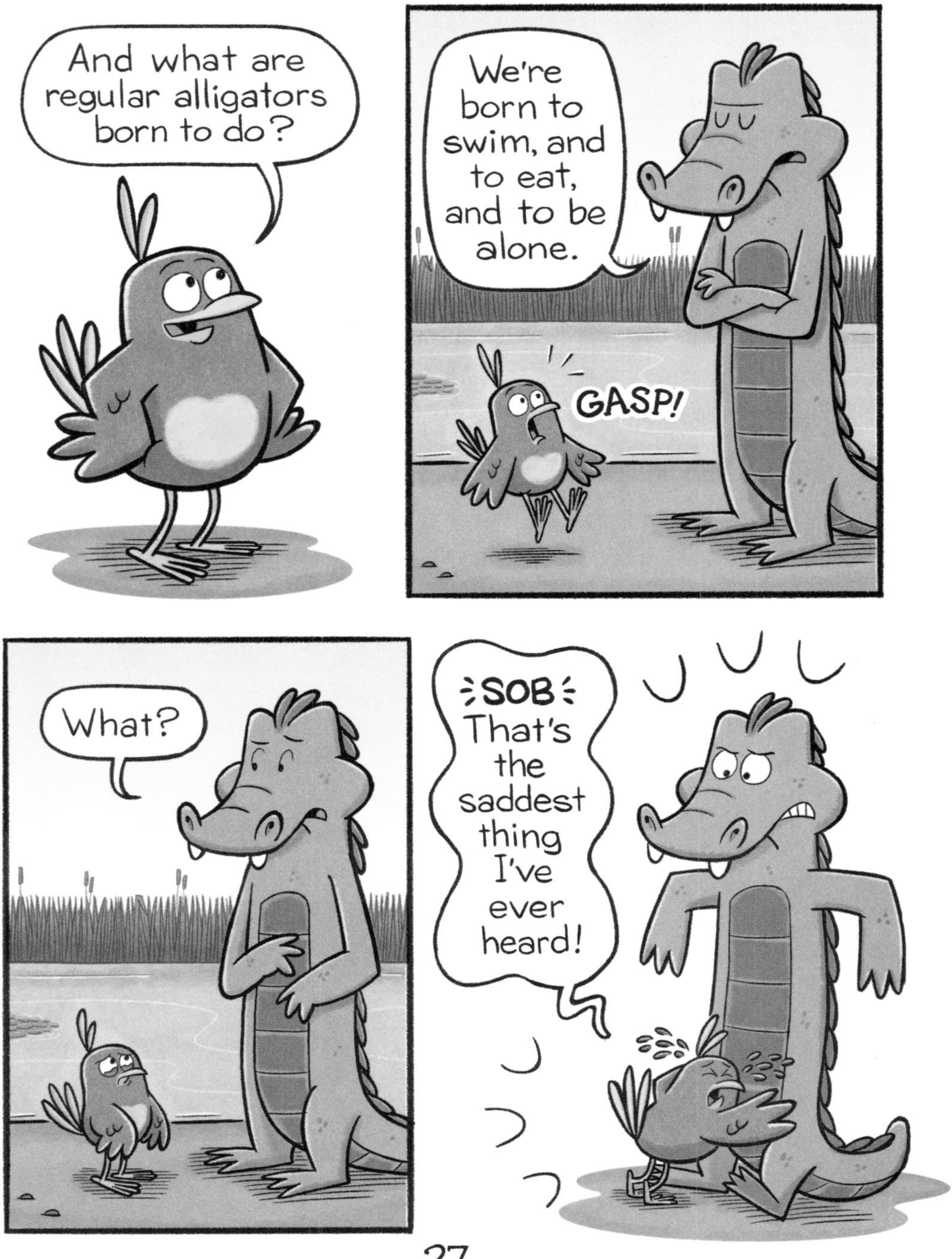
And what are regular alligators born to do?
We're born to swim, and to eat, and to be alone.
GASP!
What?
SOB
That's the saddest thing I've ever heard!

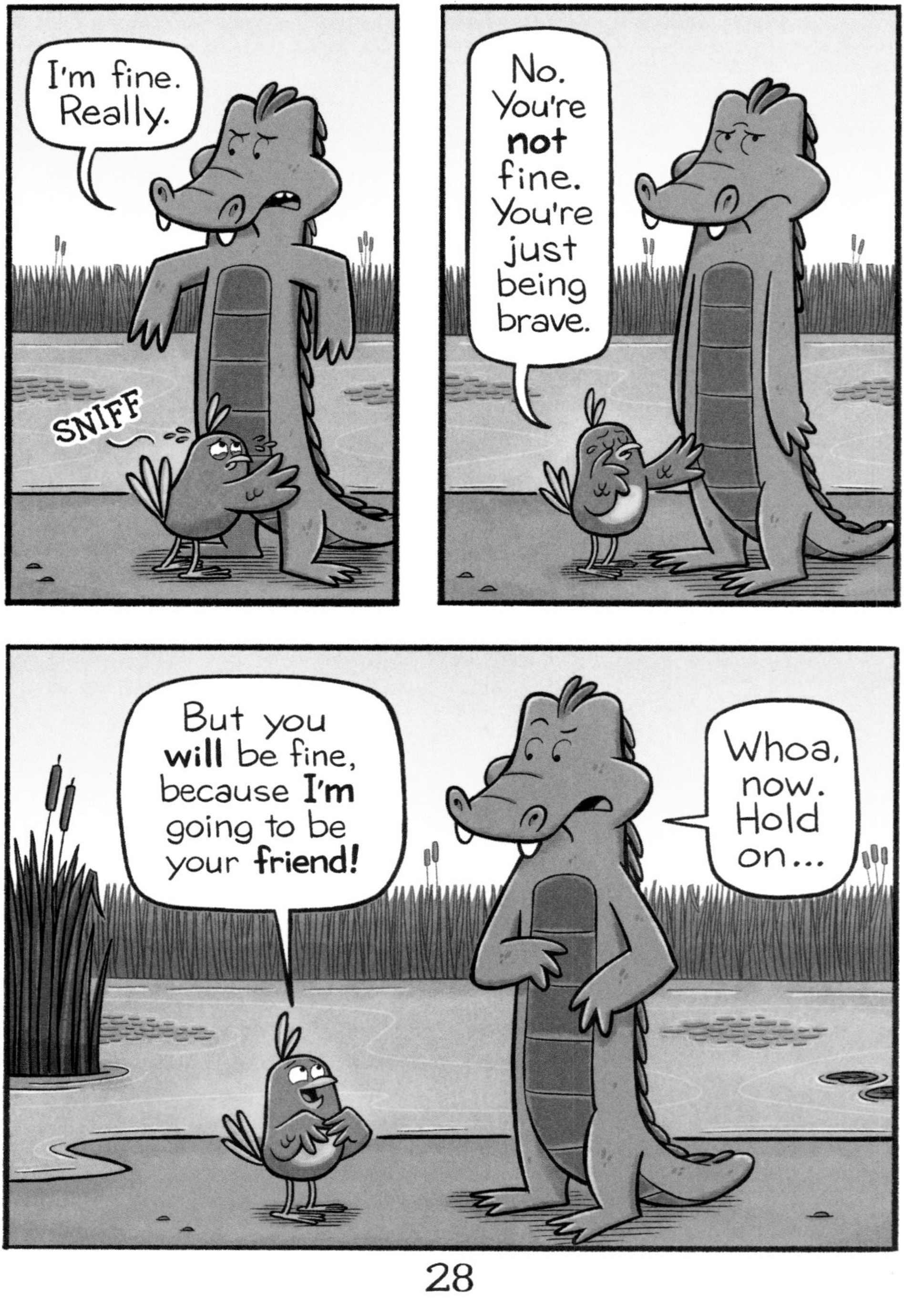
I'm fine. Really.
SNIFF
No. You're **not** fine. You're just being brave.
But you **will** be fine, because **I'm** going to be your **friend!**
Whoa, now. Hold on...

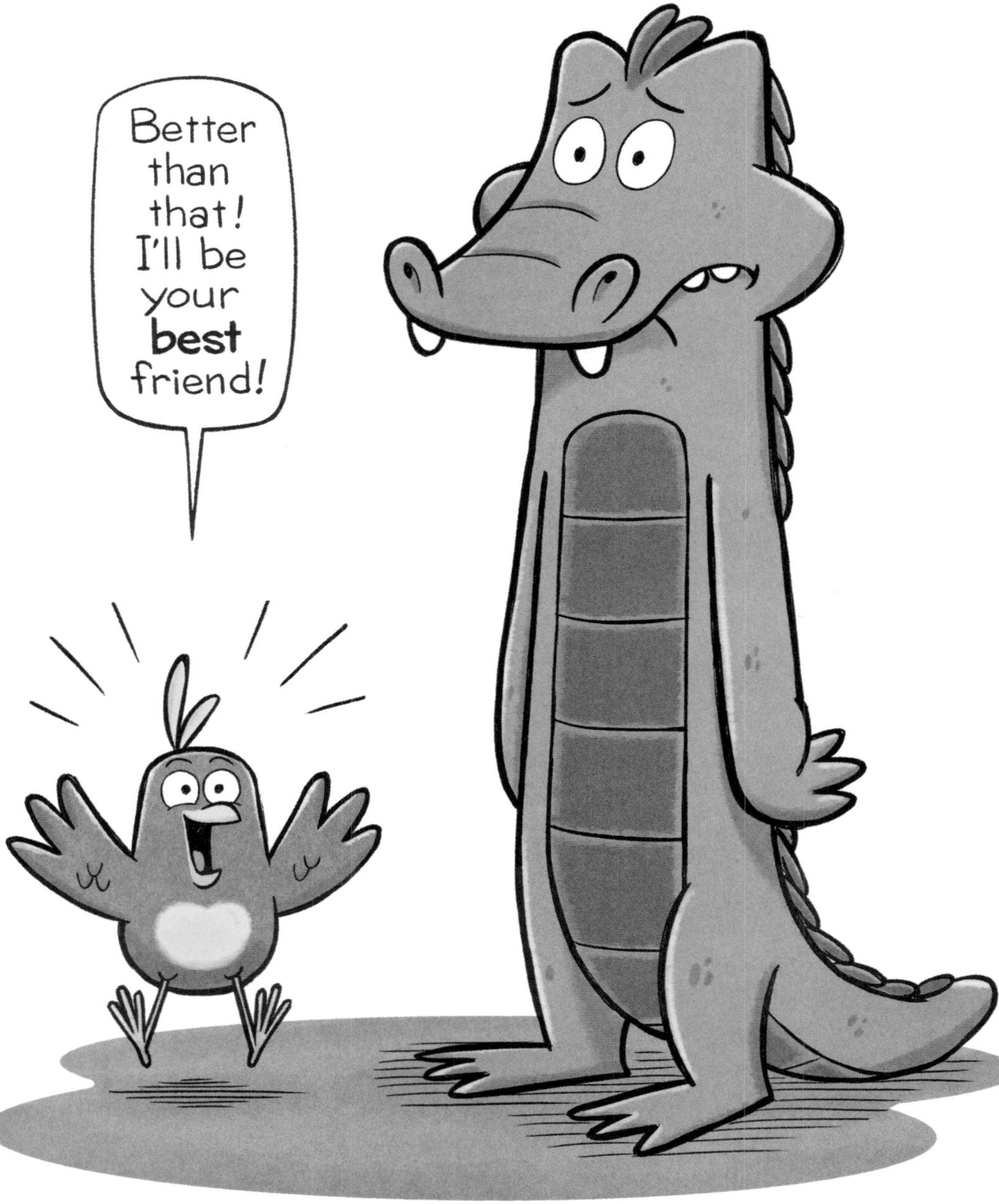
Better than that! I'll be your **best** friend!

We'll do
everything
together!

♪ Ring ♪
Ring ♪

We'll go
bike riding!

We'll go to
the movies!

We'll go on one of those baking shows!

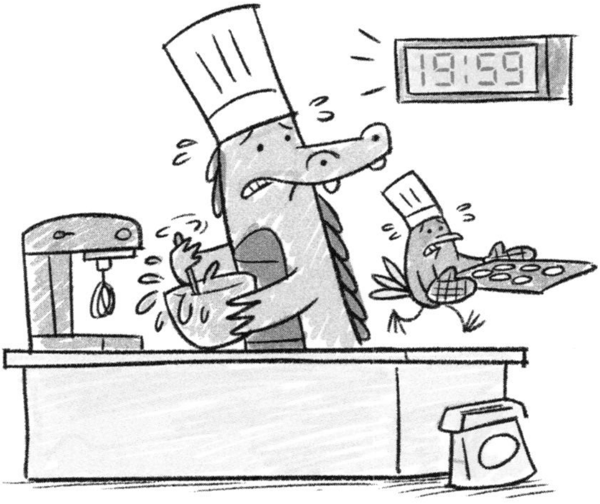
19:59

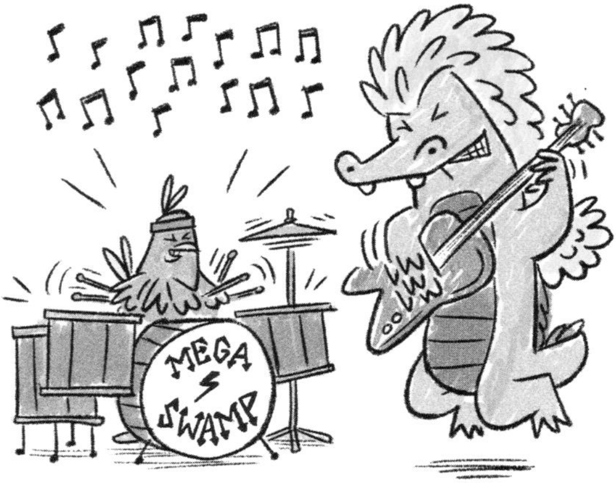
MEGA SWAMP

We'll form a rock band!

We'll solve mysteries!

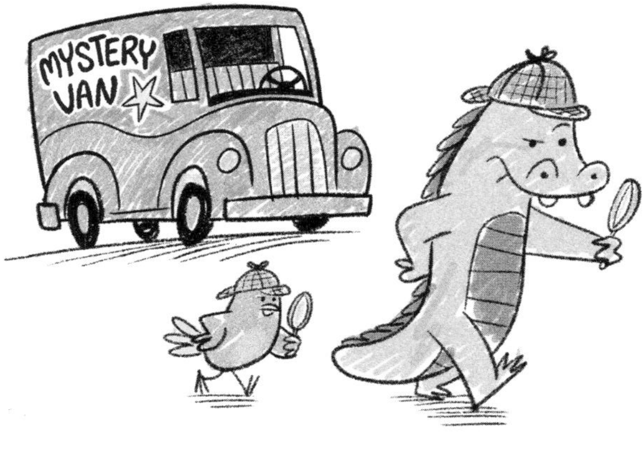
MYSTERY VAN

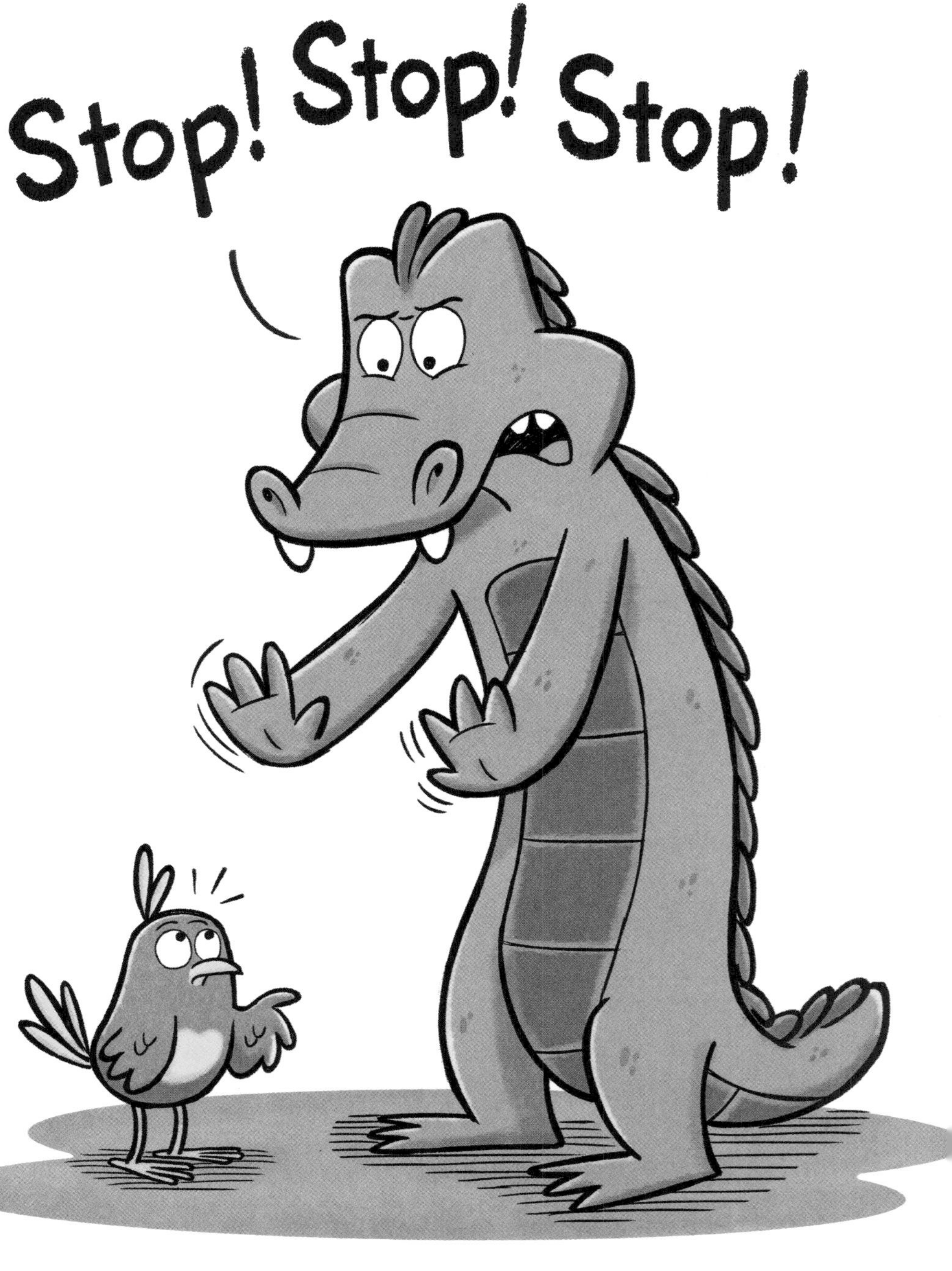
Stop! Stop! Stop!

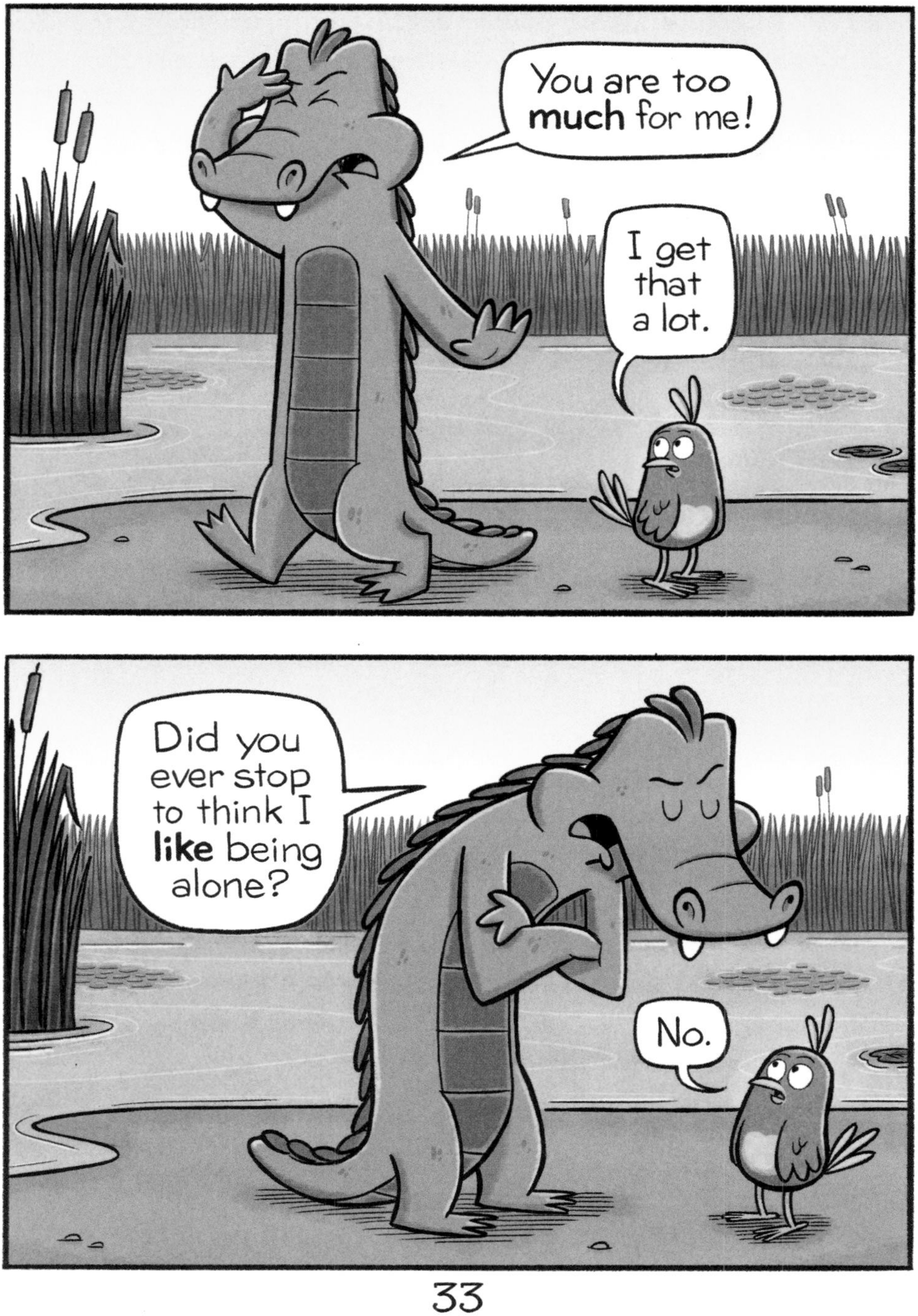
You are too **much** for me!
I get that a lot.
Did you ever stop to think I **like** being alone?
No.

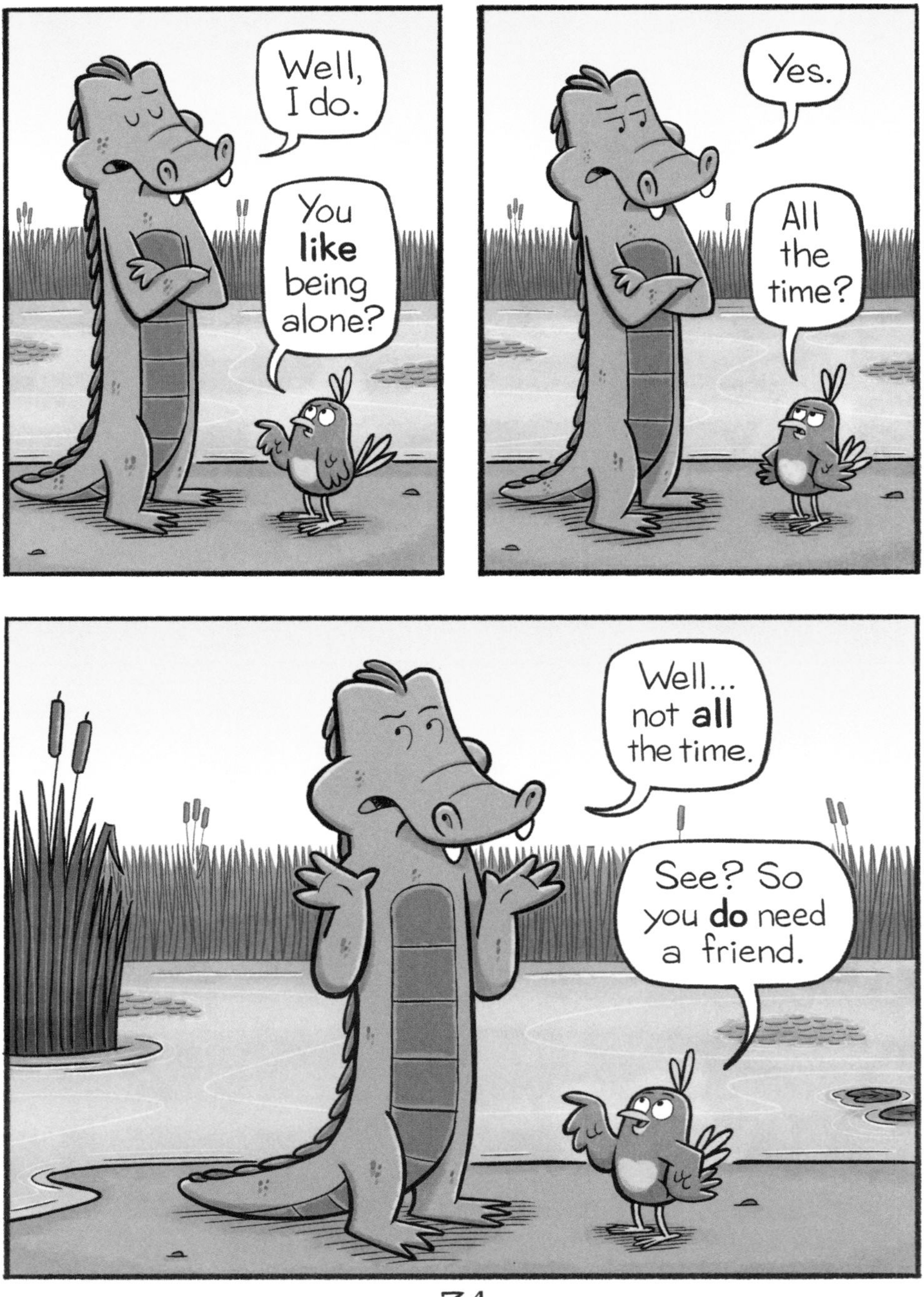
Well, I do.
You **like** being alone?
Yes.
All the time?
Well... not **all** the time.
See? So you **do** need a friend.

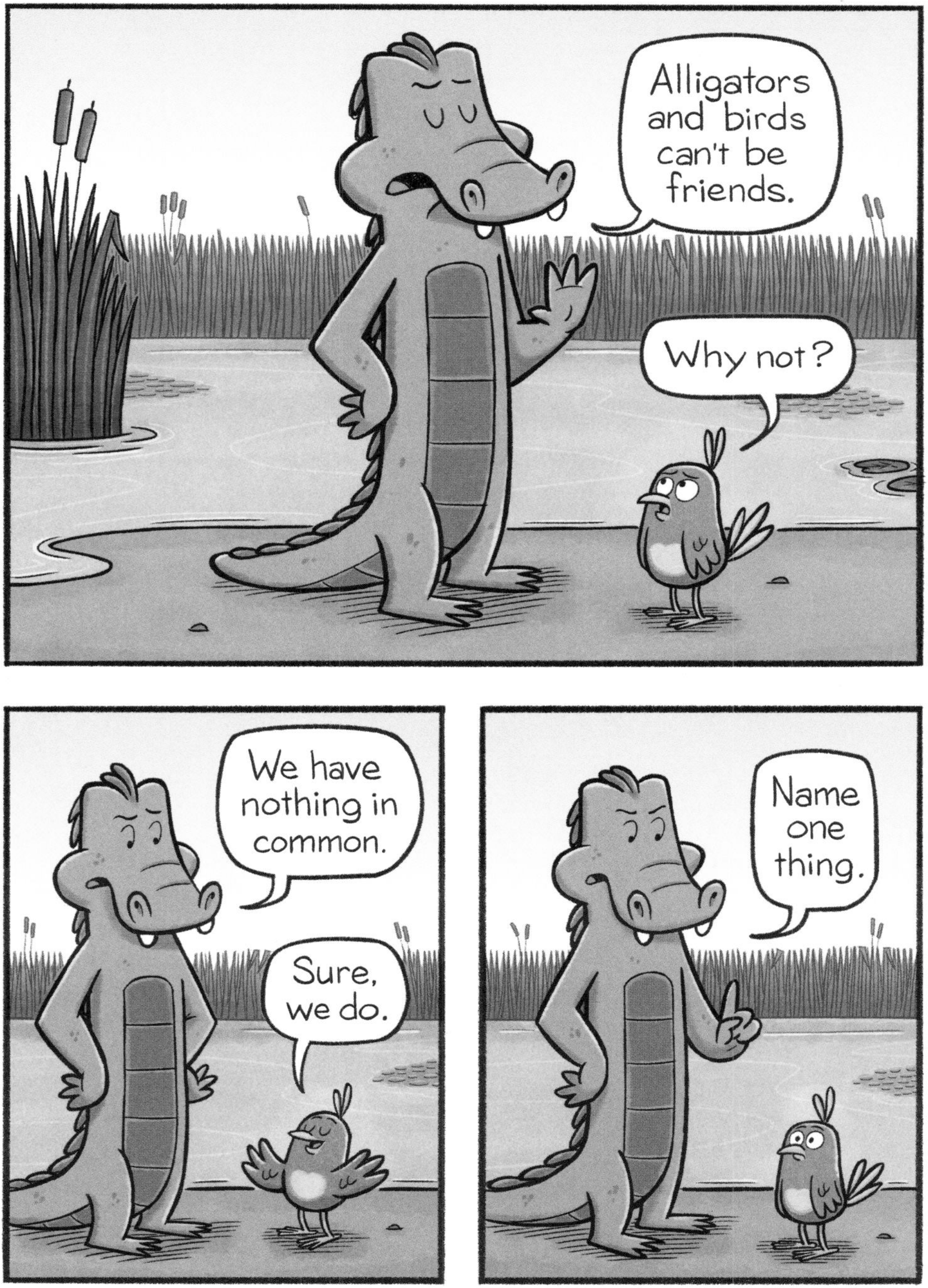
Alligators and birds can't be friends.
Why not?
We have nothing in common.
Sure, we do.
Name one thing.

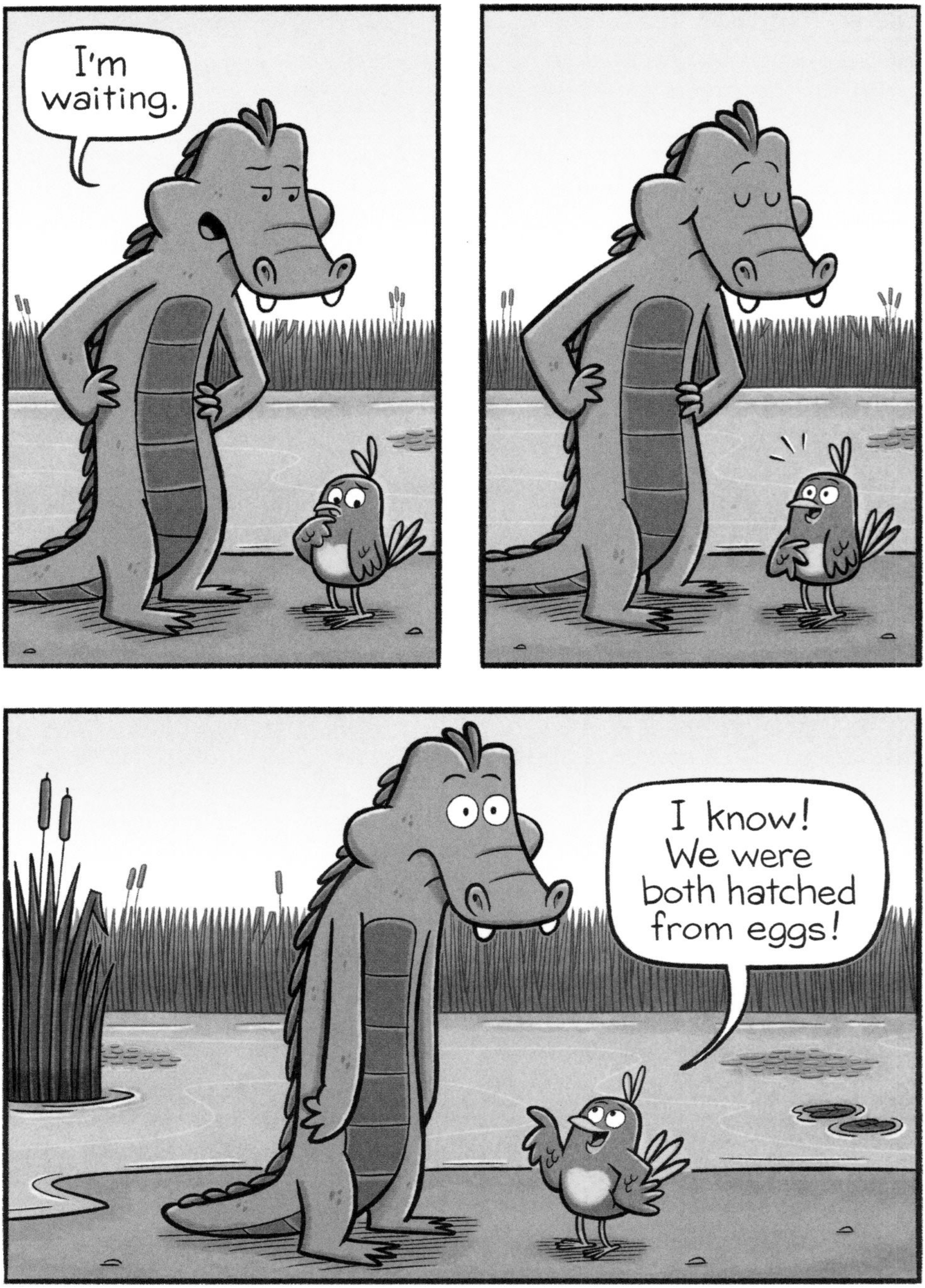
I'm waiting.
I know! We were both hatched from eggs!

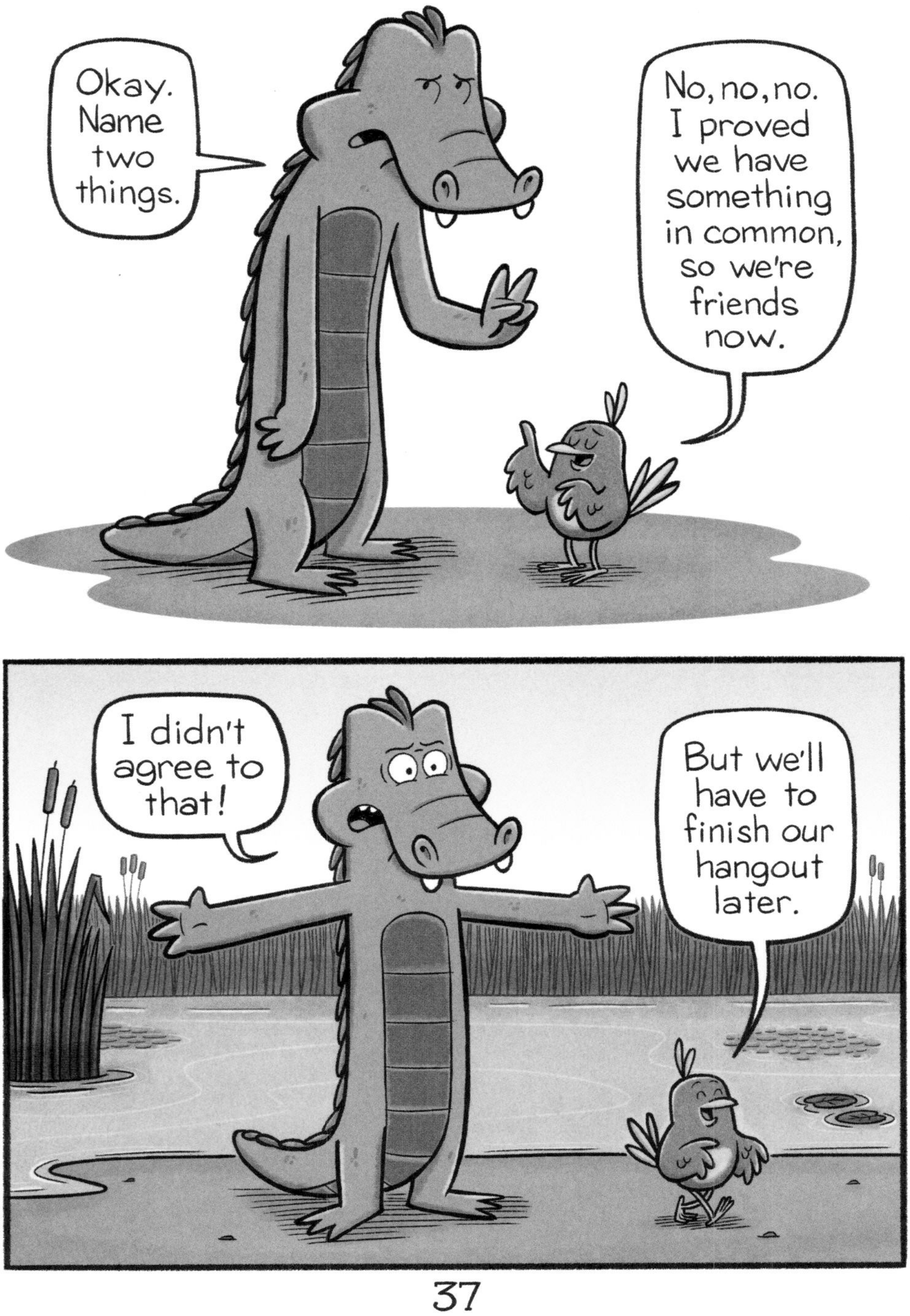
Okay. Name two things.
No, no, no. I proved we have something in common, so we're friends now.
I didn't agree to that!
But we'll have to finish our hangout later.

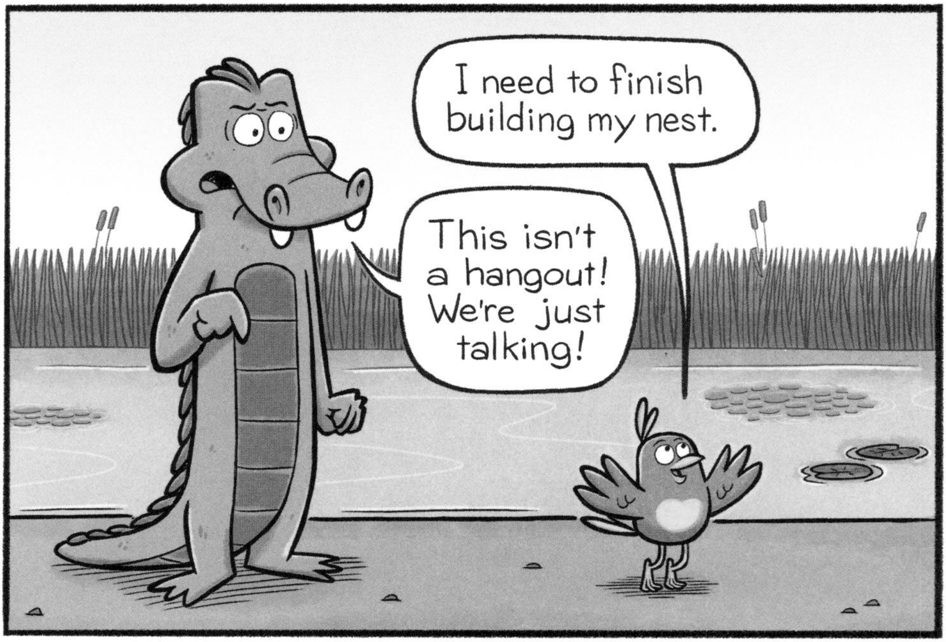
I need to finish building my nest.
This isn't a hangout! We're just talking!

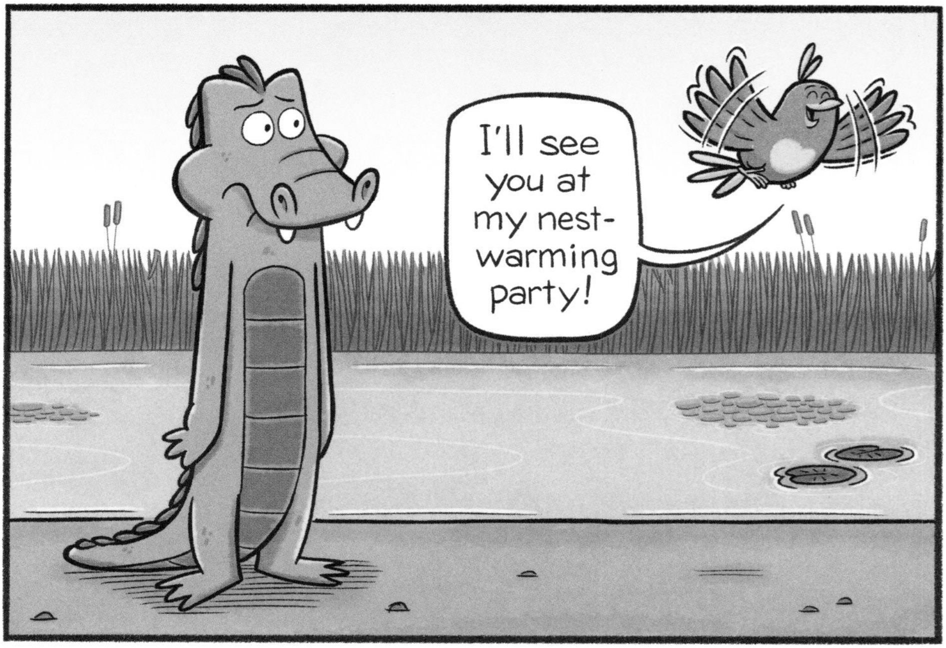
I'll see you at my nest-warming party!

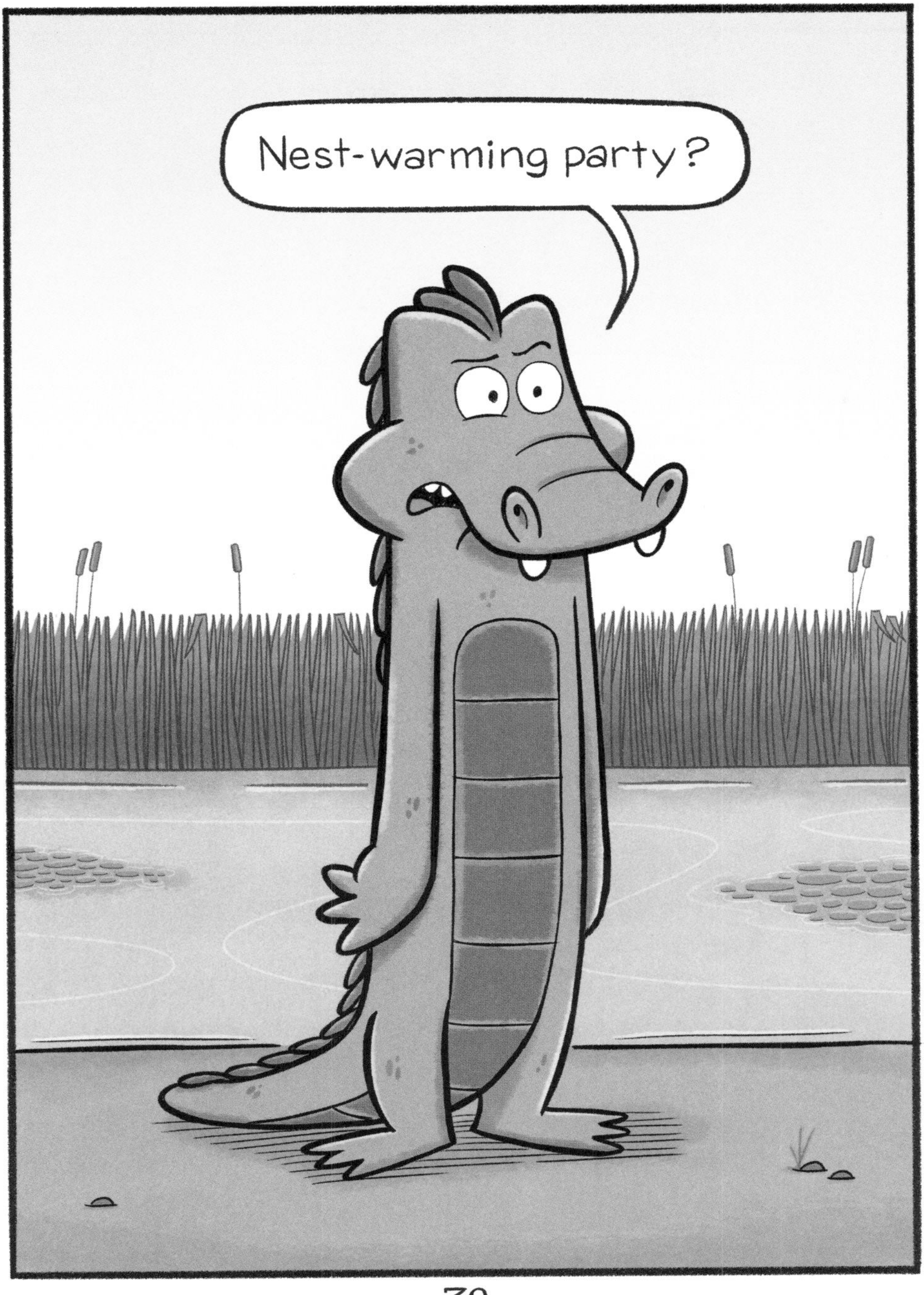
Nest-warming party?

Three

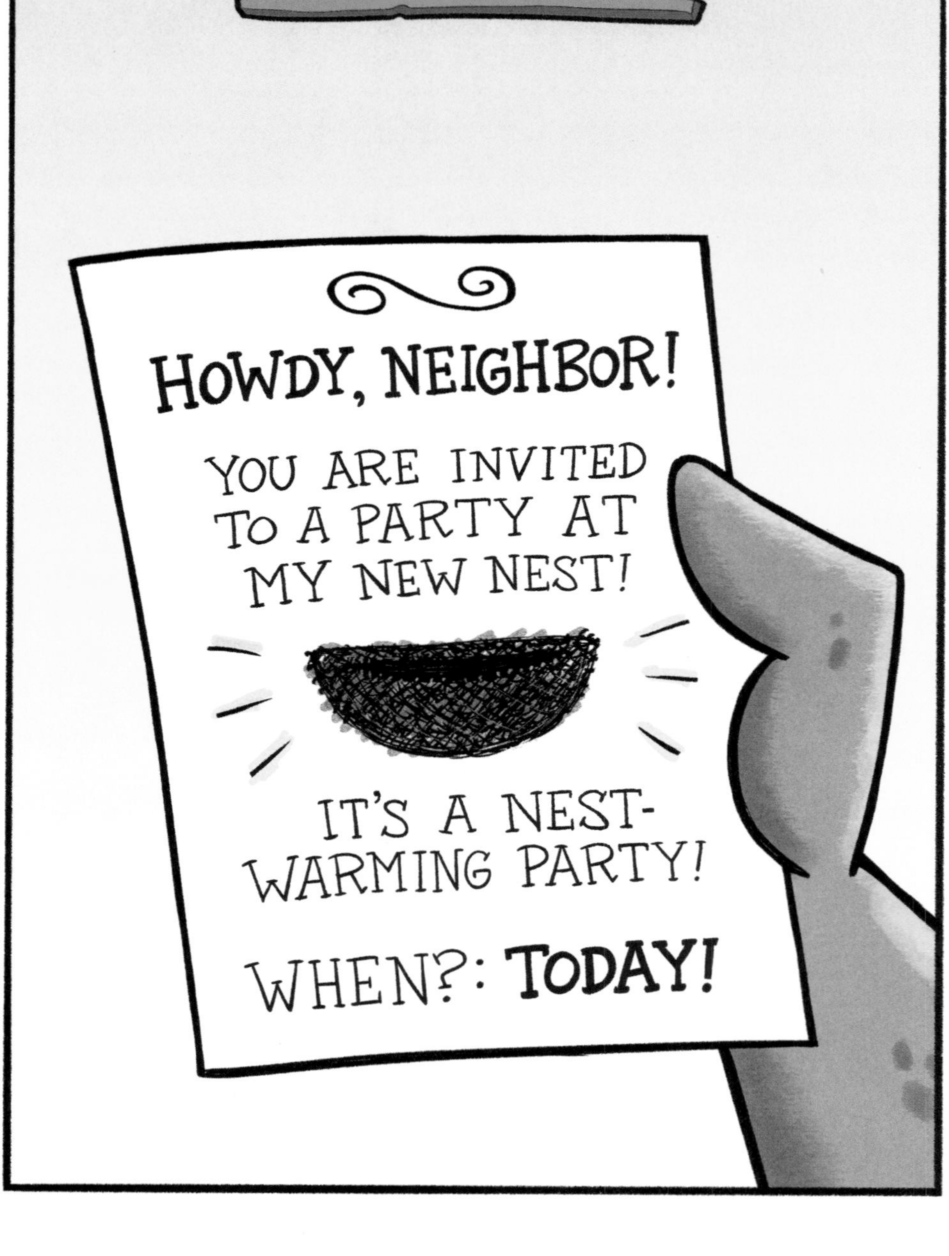
HOWDY, NEIGHBOR!
YOU ARE INVITED TO A PARTY AT MY NEW NEST!
IT'S A NEST-WARMING PARTY!
WHEN?: **TODAY!**

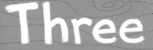

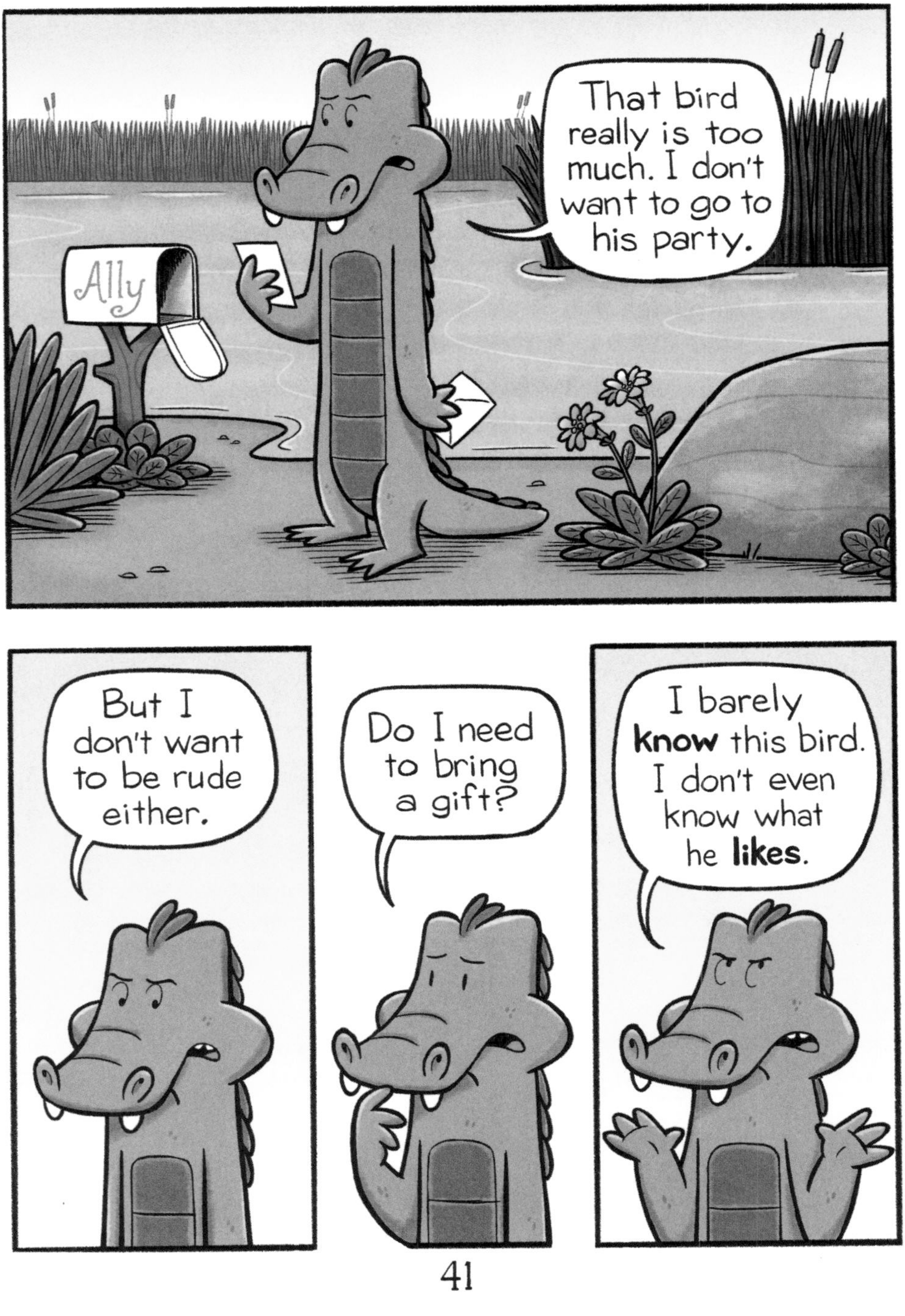

Ally
That bird really is too much. I don't want to go to his party.
But I don't want to be rude either.
Do I need to bring a gift?
I barely **know** this bird. I don't even know what he **likes**.

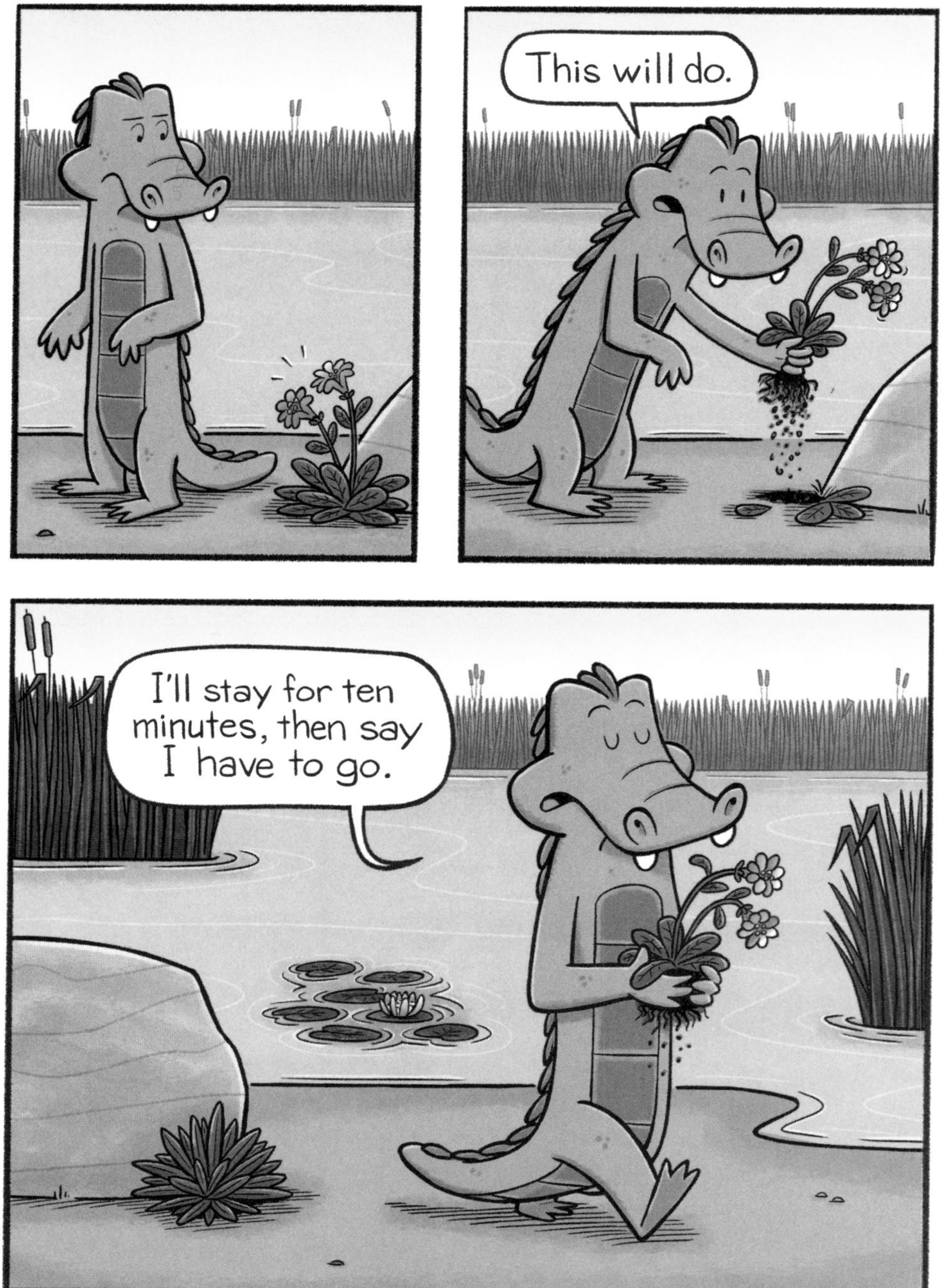
This will do.
I'll stay for ten minutes, then say I have to go.

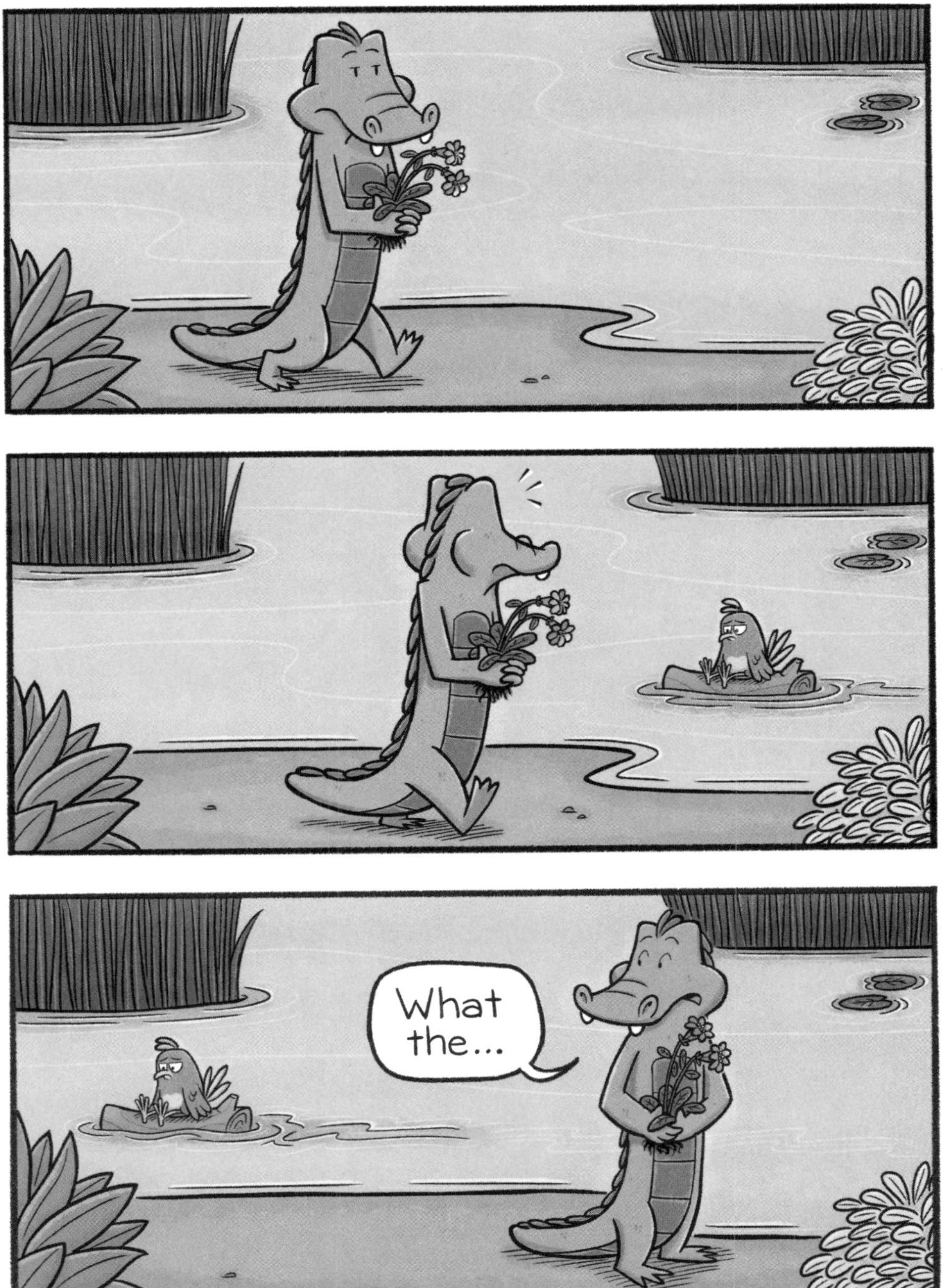
What the...

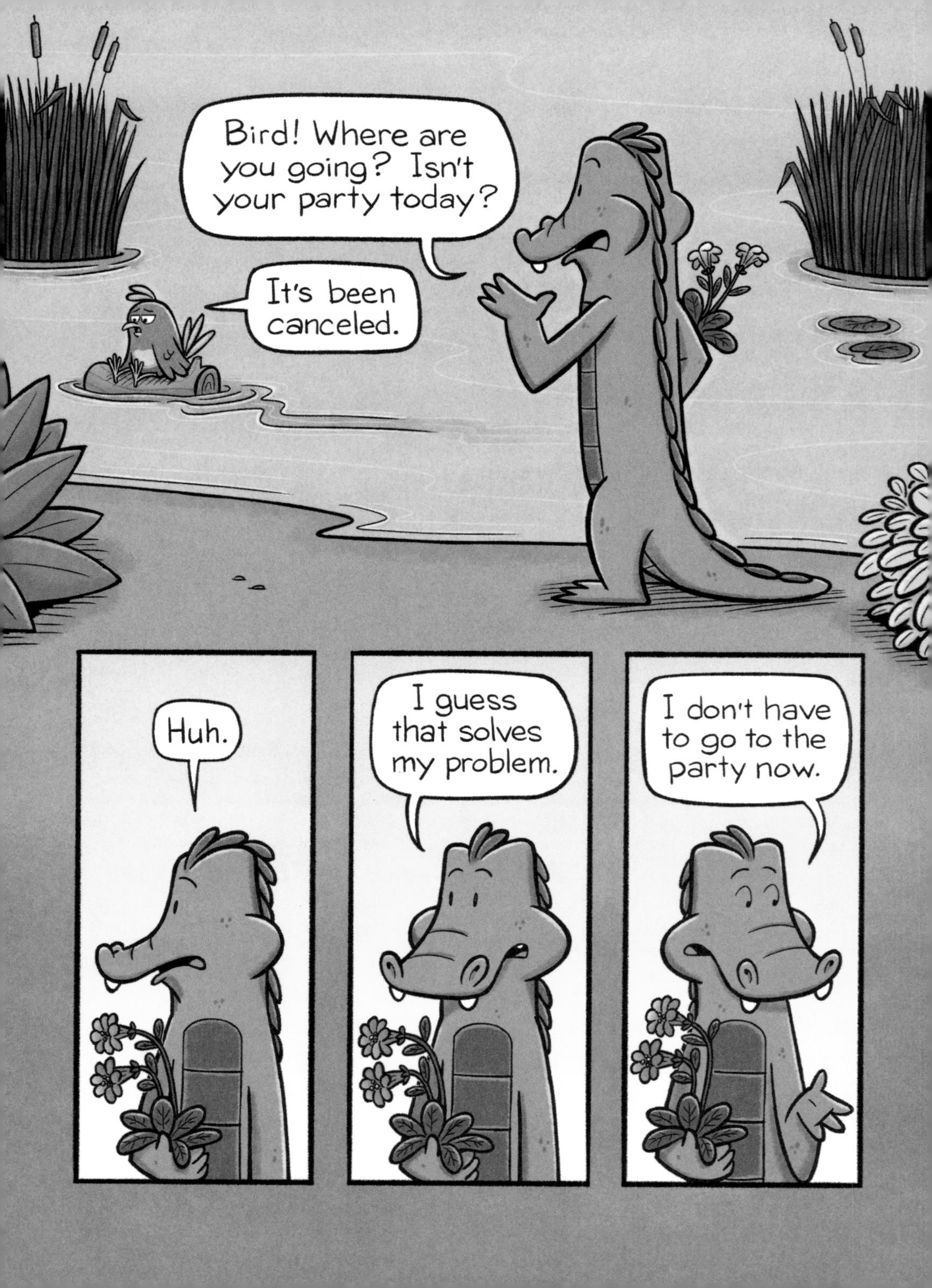
Bird! Where are you going? Isn't your party today?
It's been canceled.
Huh.
I guess that solves my problem.
I don't have to go to the party now.

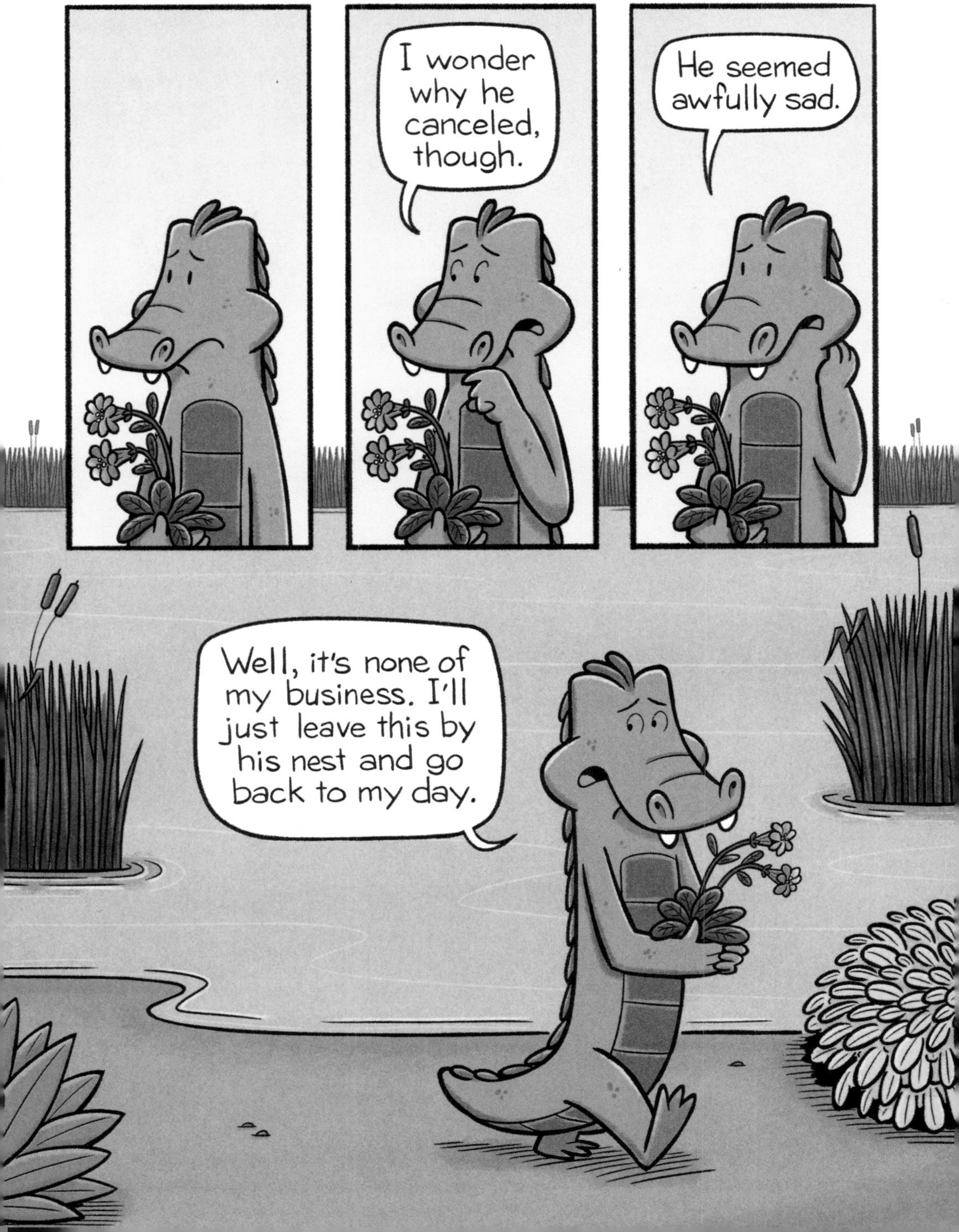
I wonder why he canceled, though.
He seemed awfully sad.
Well, it's none of my business. I'll just leave this by his nest and go back to my day.

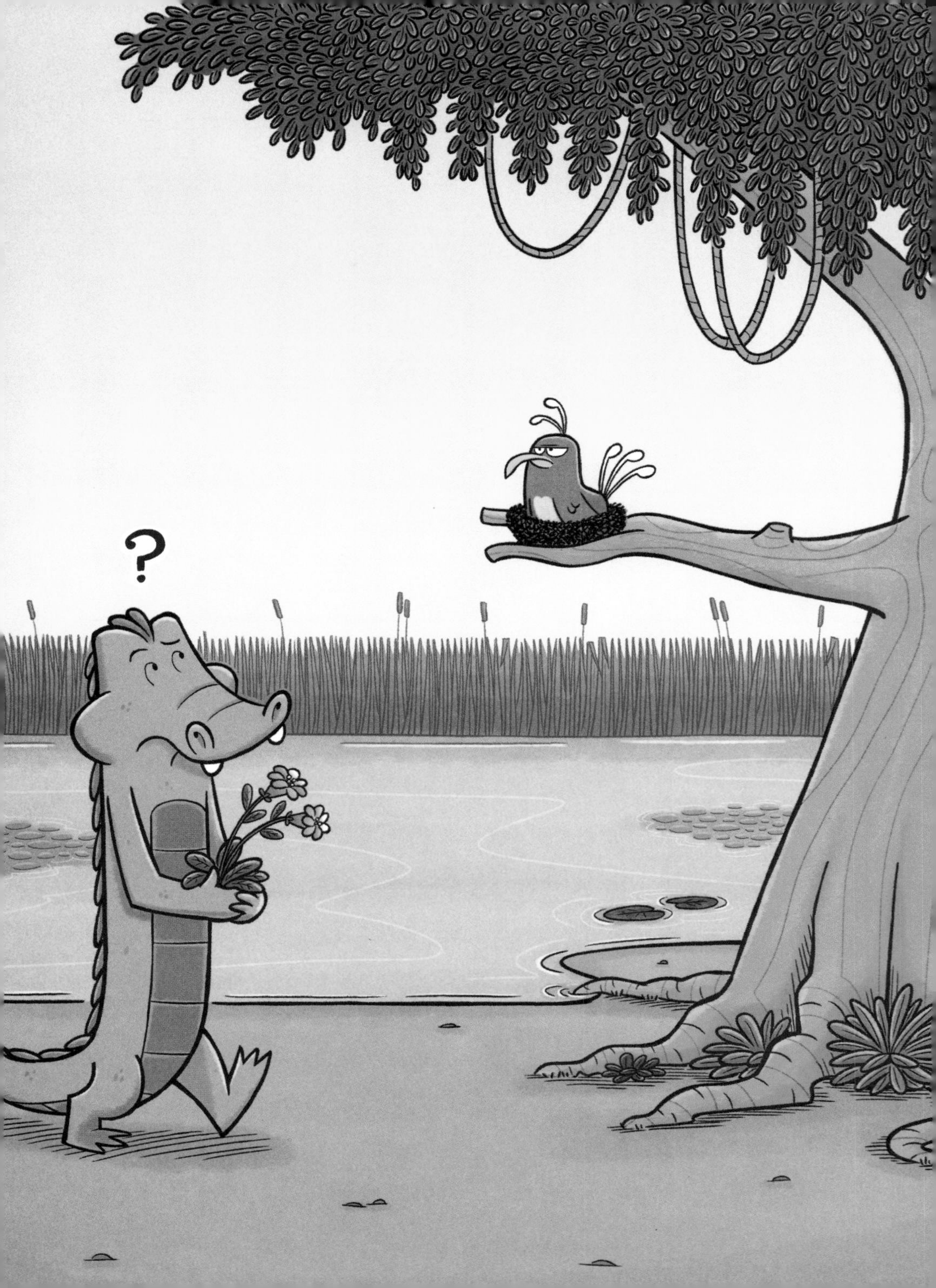
?

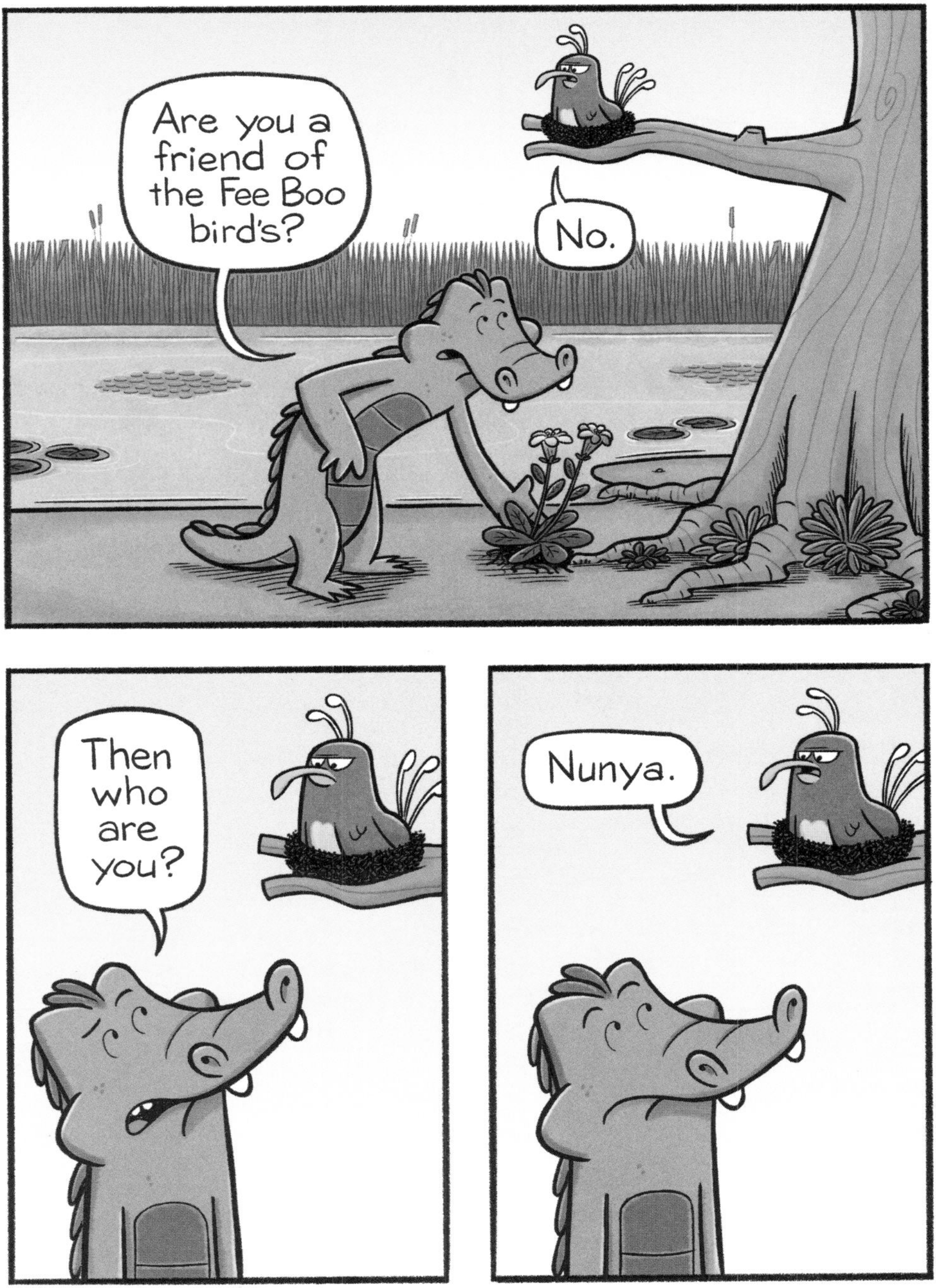
Are you a friend of the Fee Boo bird's?
No.
Then who are you?
Nunya.

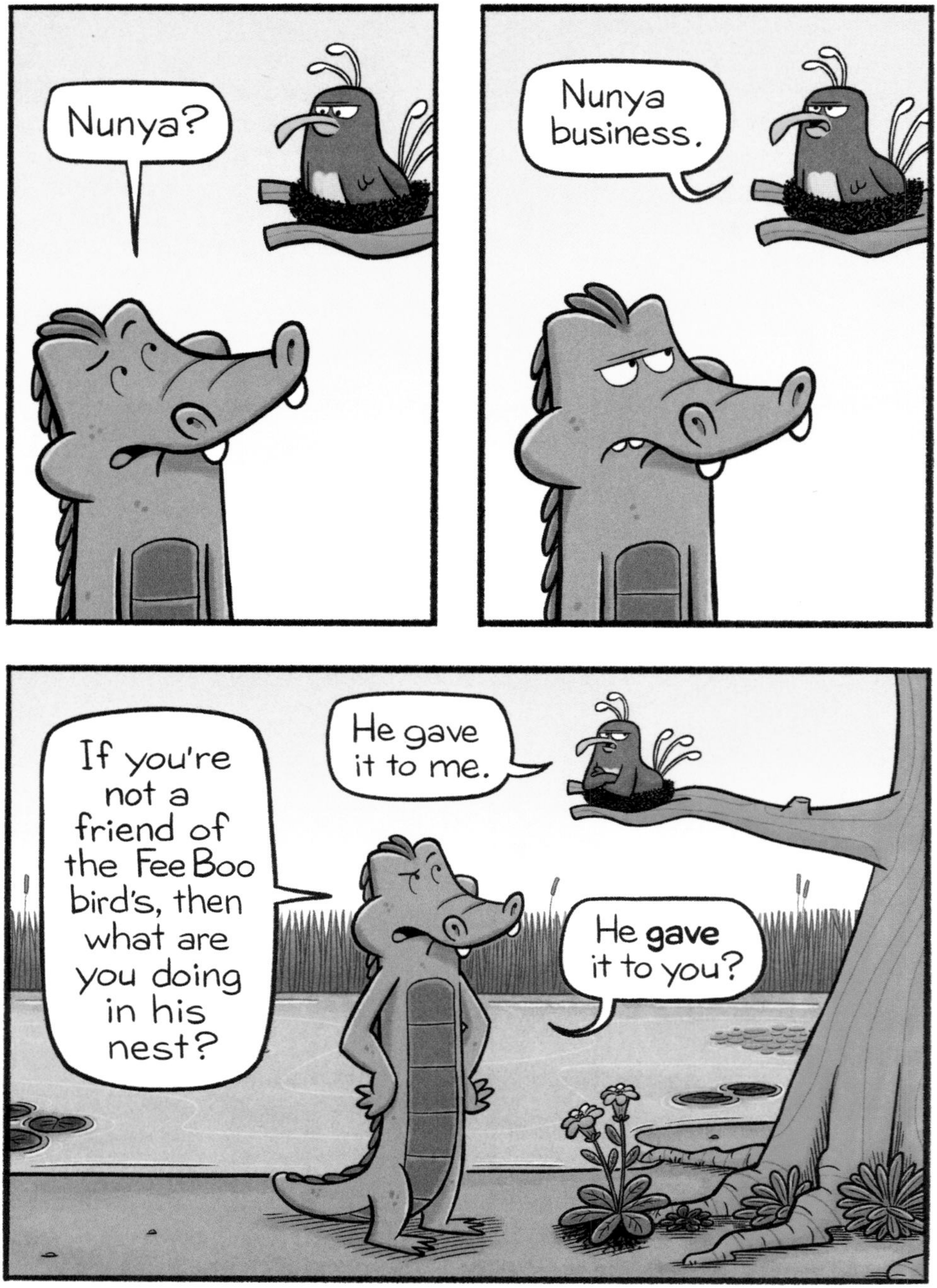
Nunya?
Nunya business.
If you're not a friend of the Fee Boo bird's, then what are you doing in his nest?
He gave it to me.
He **gave** it to you?

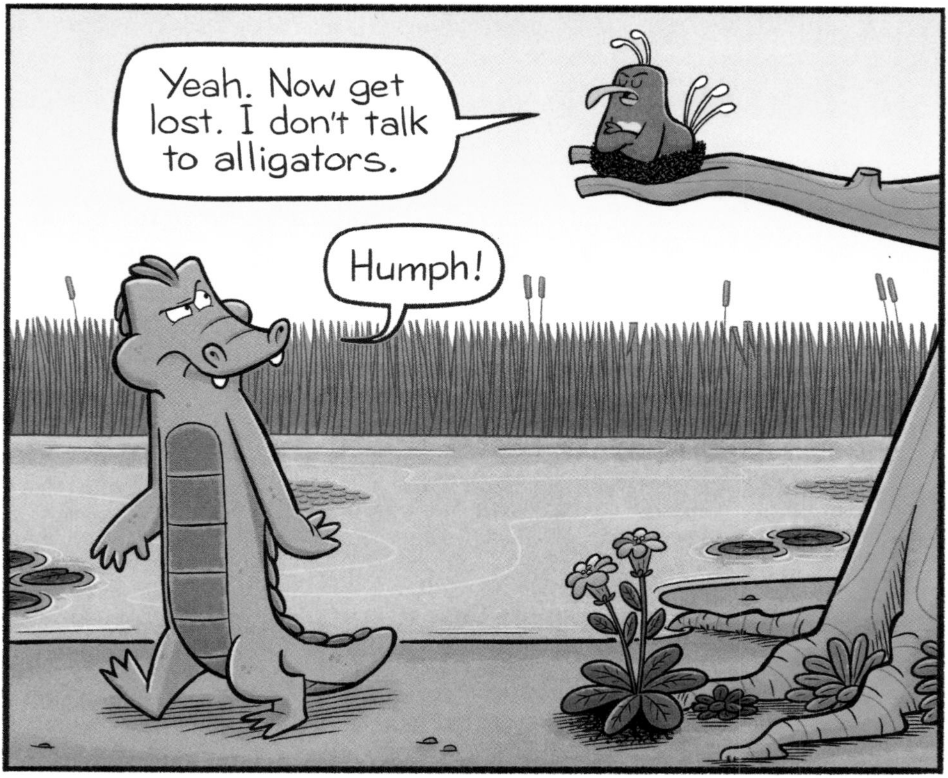
Yeah. Now get lost. I don't talk to alligators.
Humph!

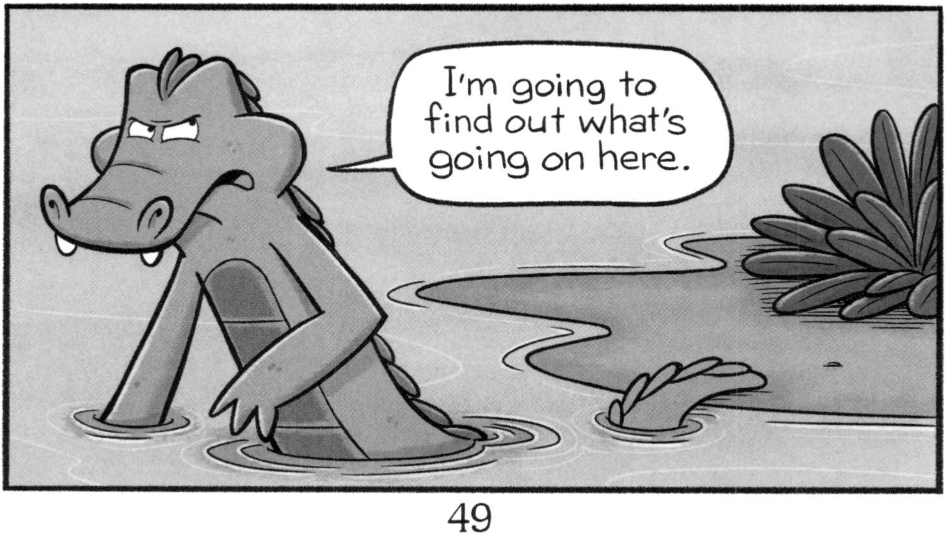
I'm going to find out what's going on here.

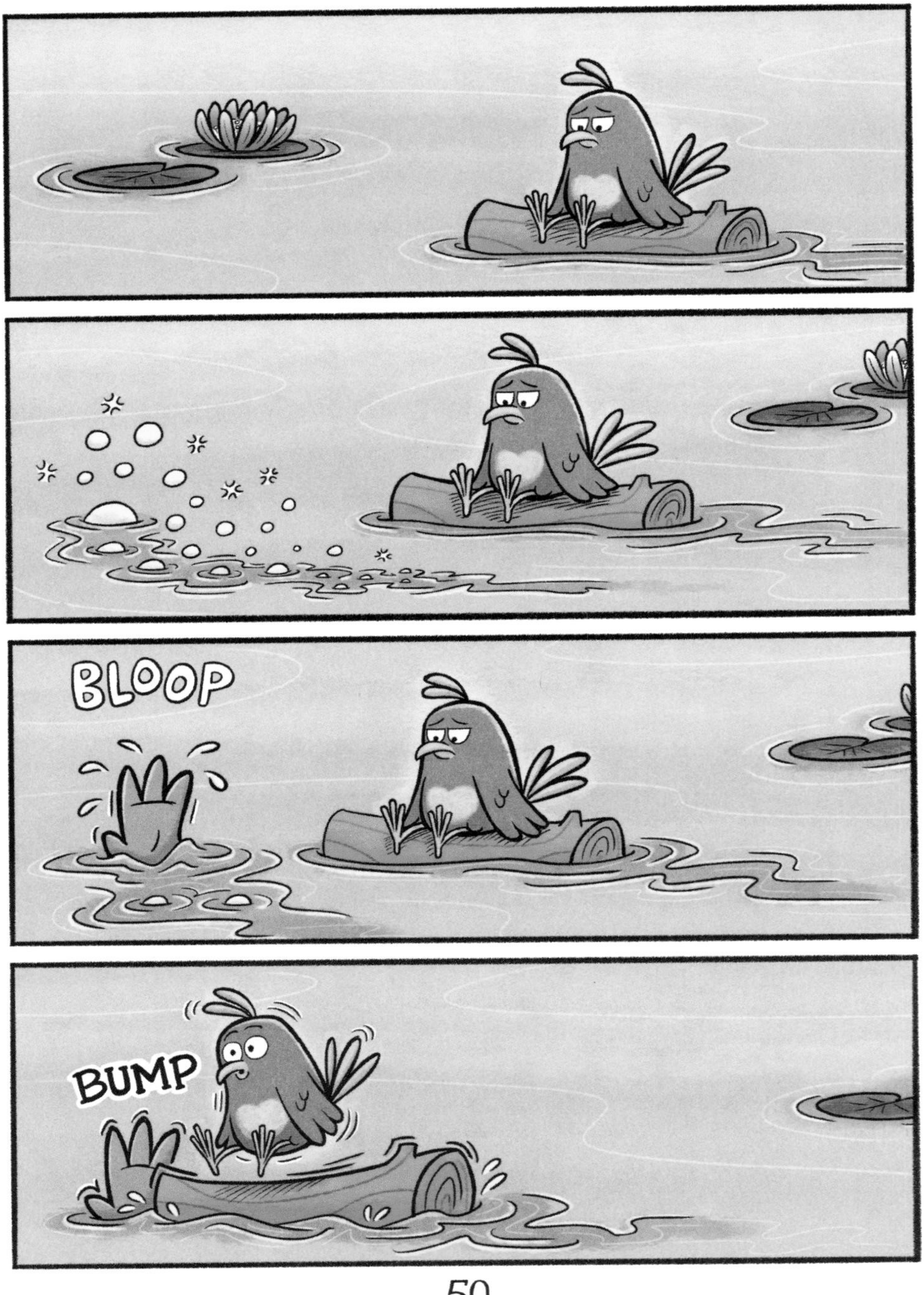
BLOOP
BUMP

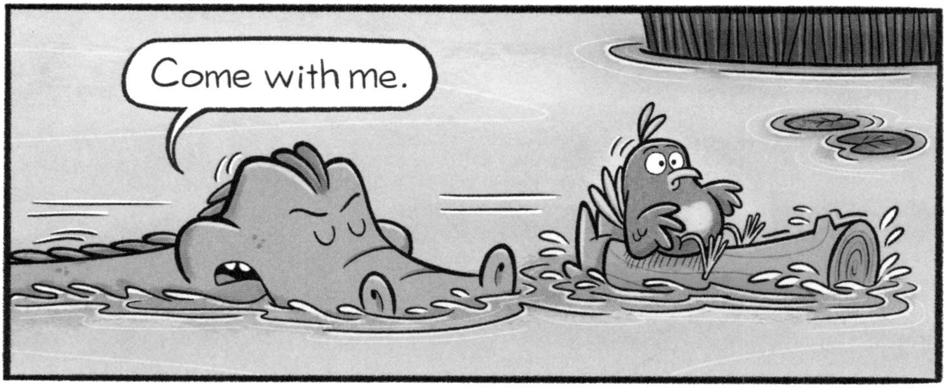
Come with me.

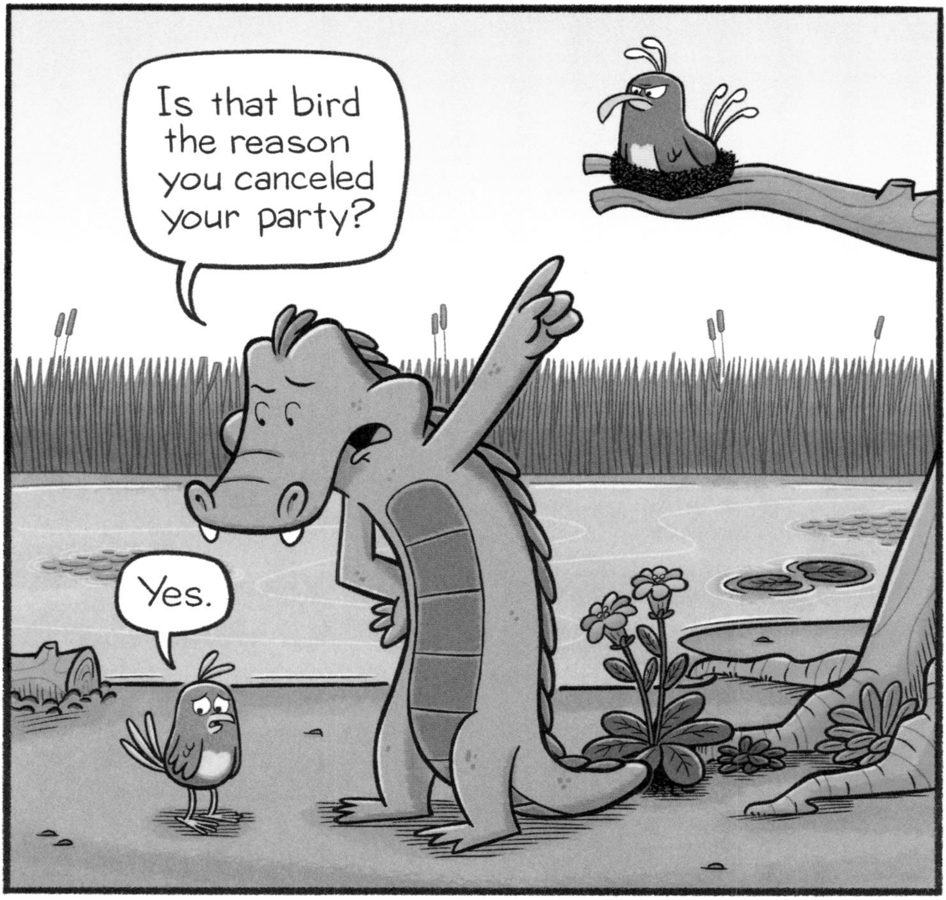
Is that bird the reason you canceled your party?
Yes.

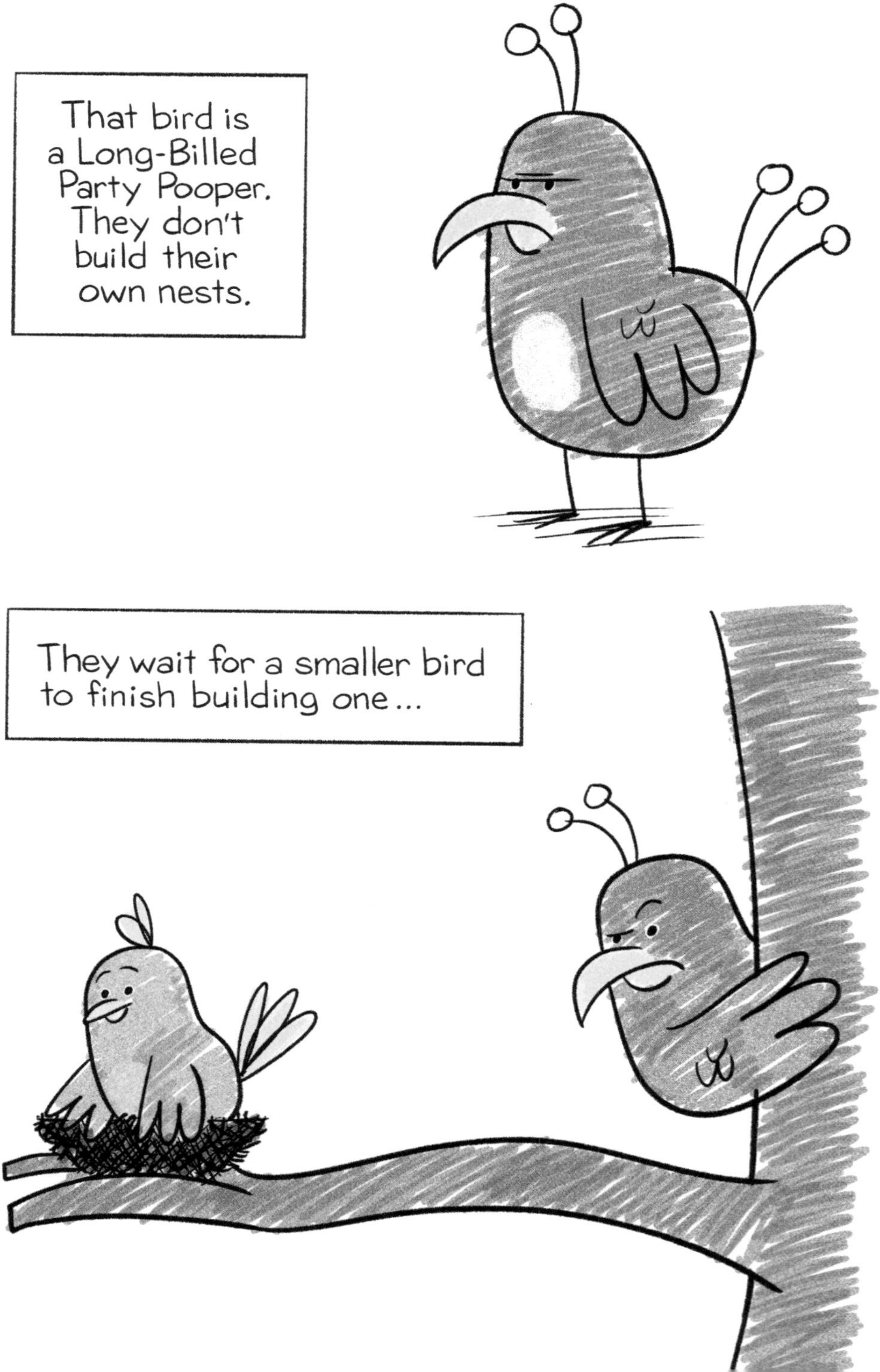
That bird is a Long-Billed Party Pooper. They don't build their own nests.
They wait for a smaller bird to finish building one...

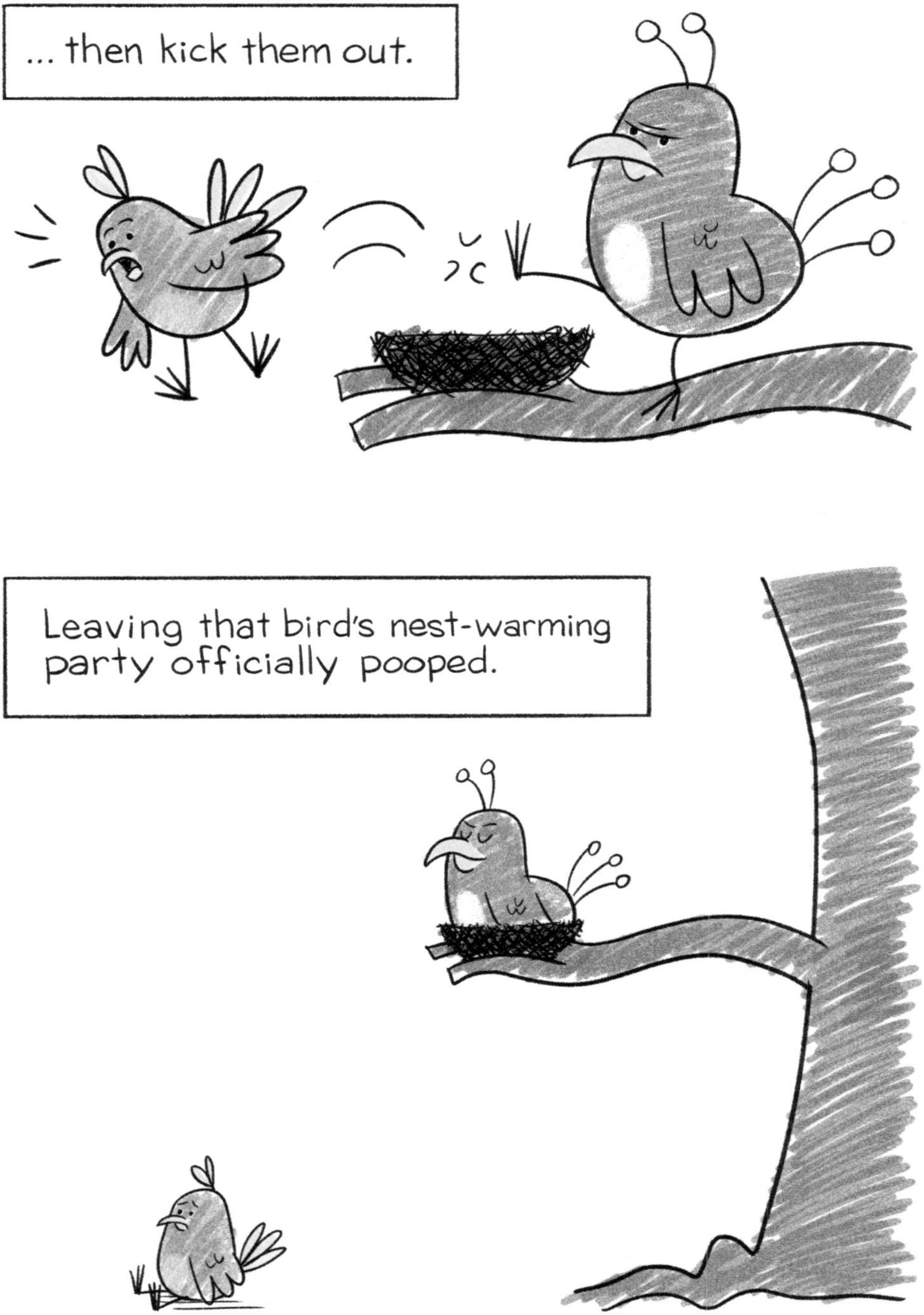
... then kick them out.
Leaving that bird's nest-warming party officially pooped.

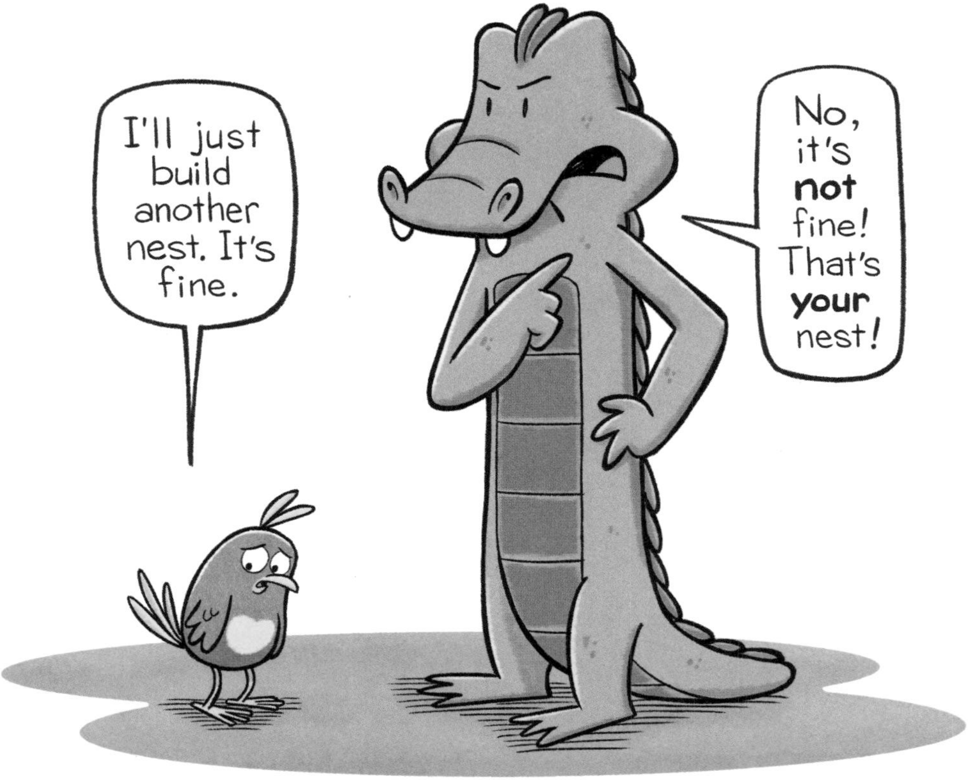
I'll just build another nest. It's fine.
No, it's **not** fine! That's **your** nest!

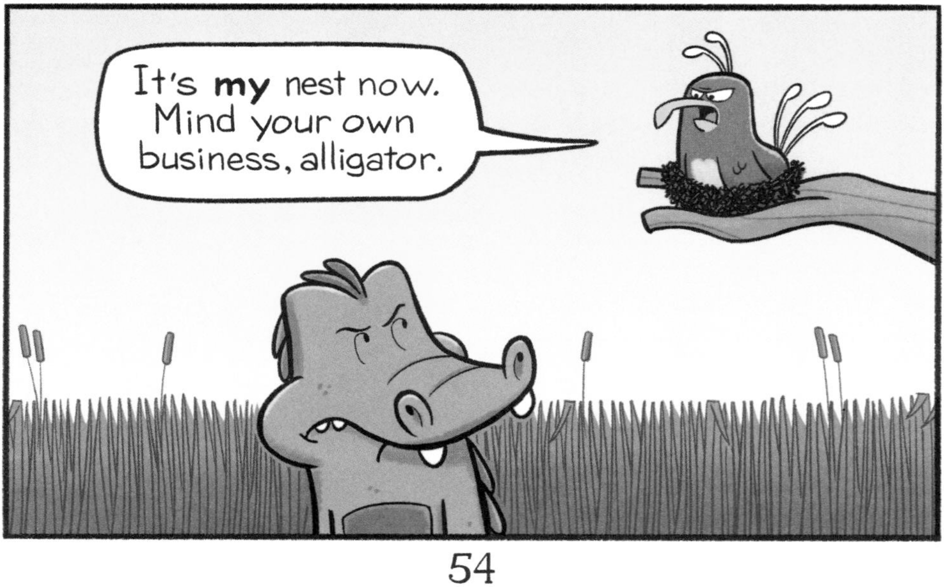
It's **my** nest now. Mind your own business, alligator.

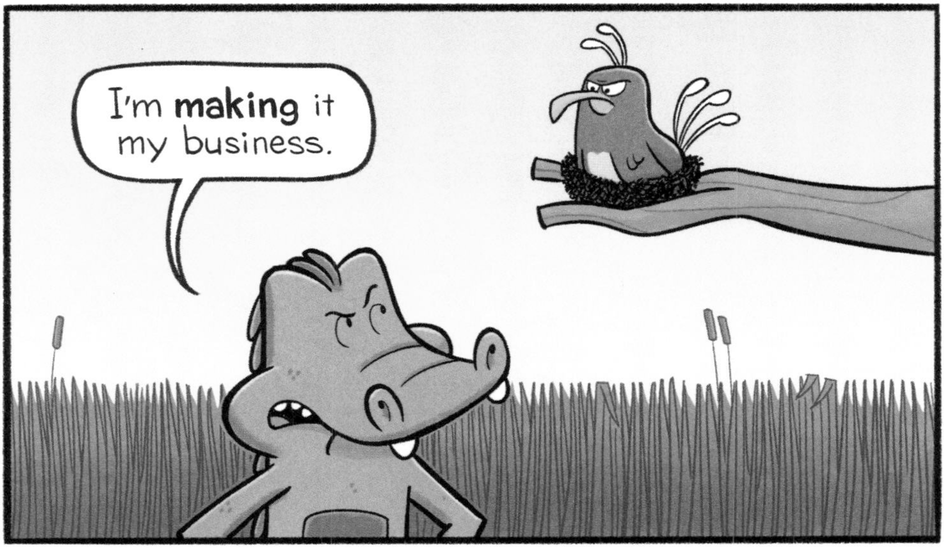
I'm **making** it my business.

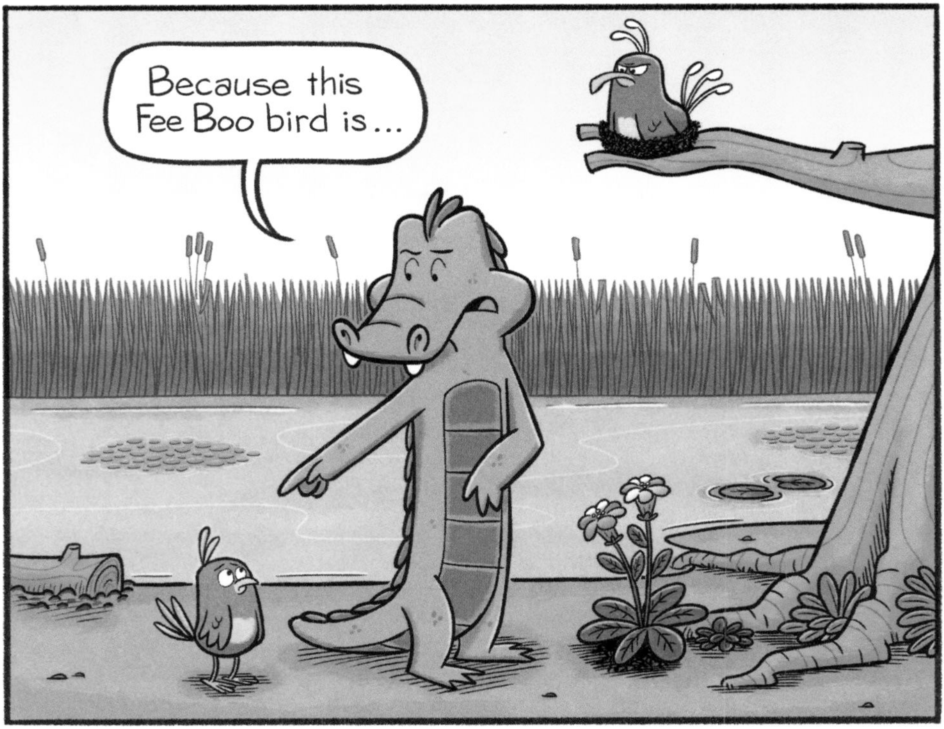
Because this Fee Boo bird is...

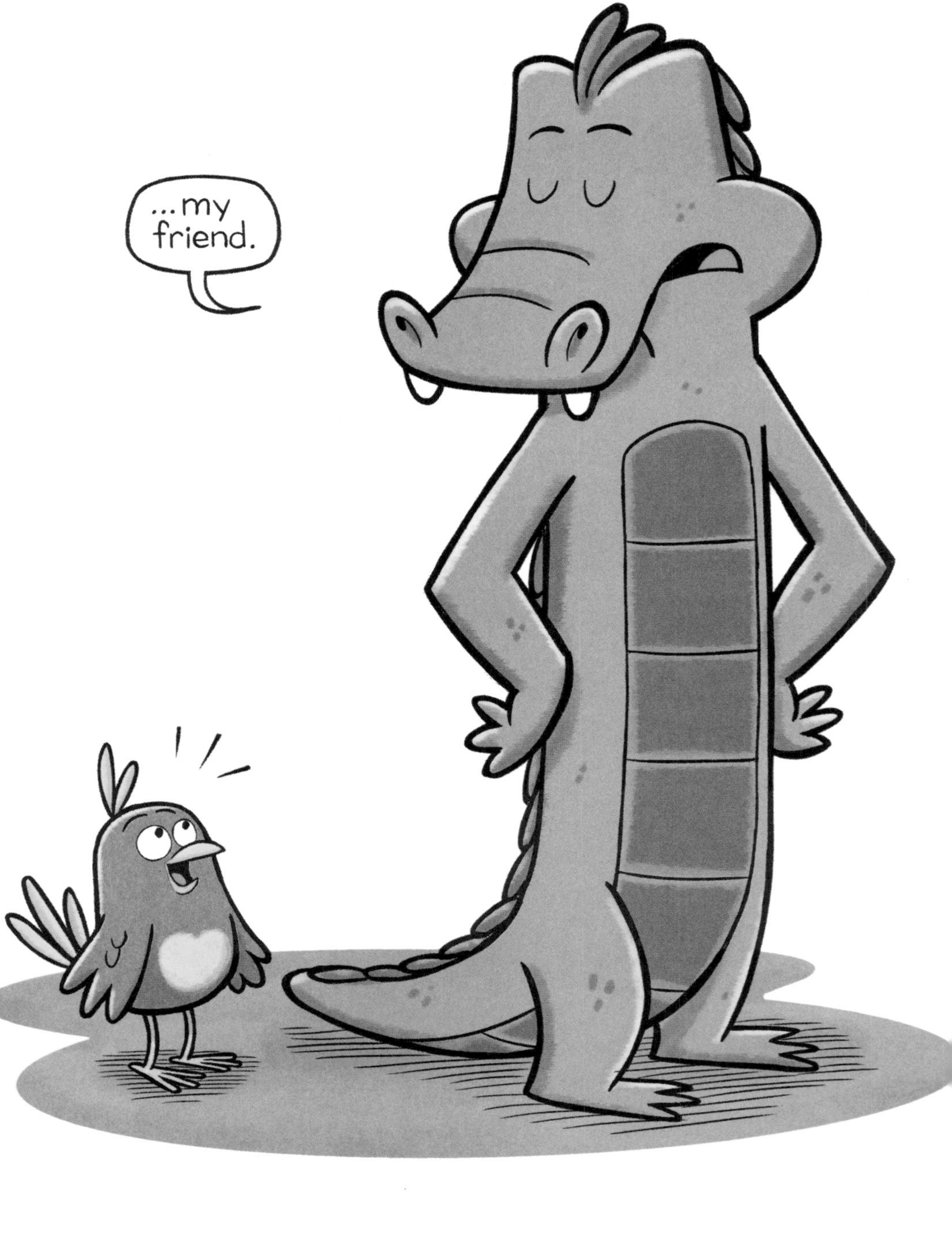
...my friend.

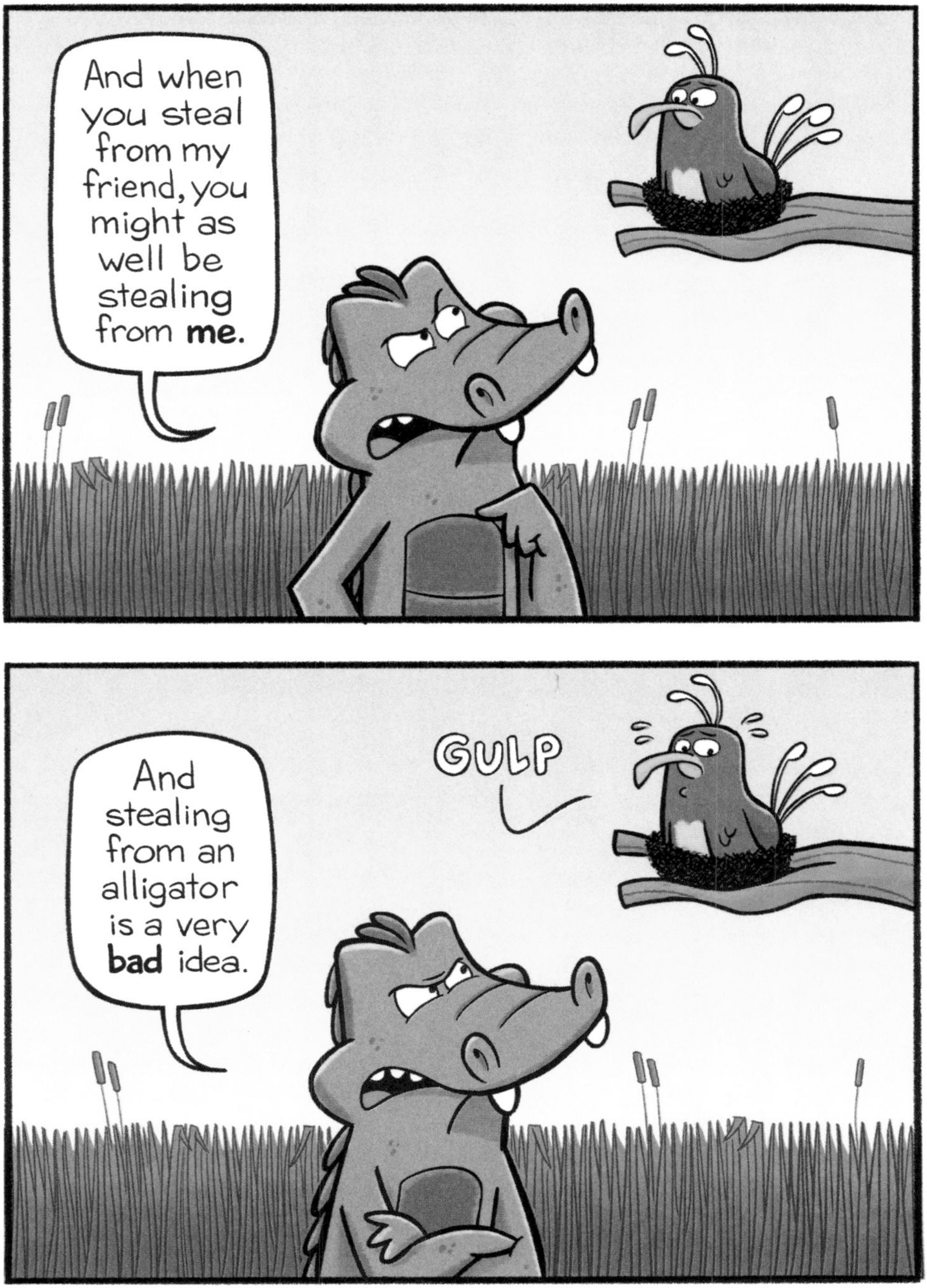
And when you steal from my friend, you might as well be stealing from **me.**
And stealing from an alligator is a very **bad** idea.
GULP

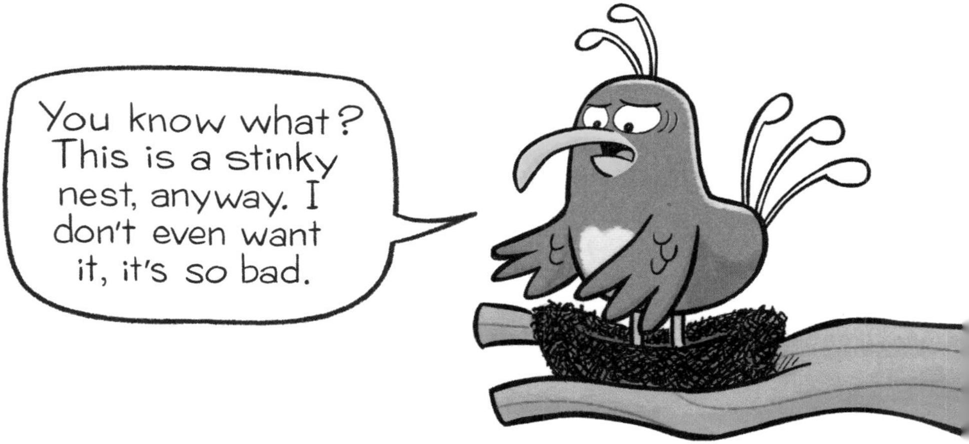
You know what? This is a stinky nest, anyway. I don't even want it, it's so bad.

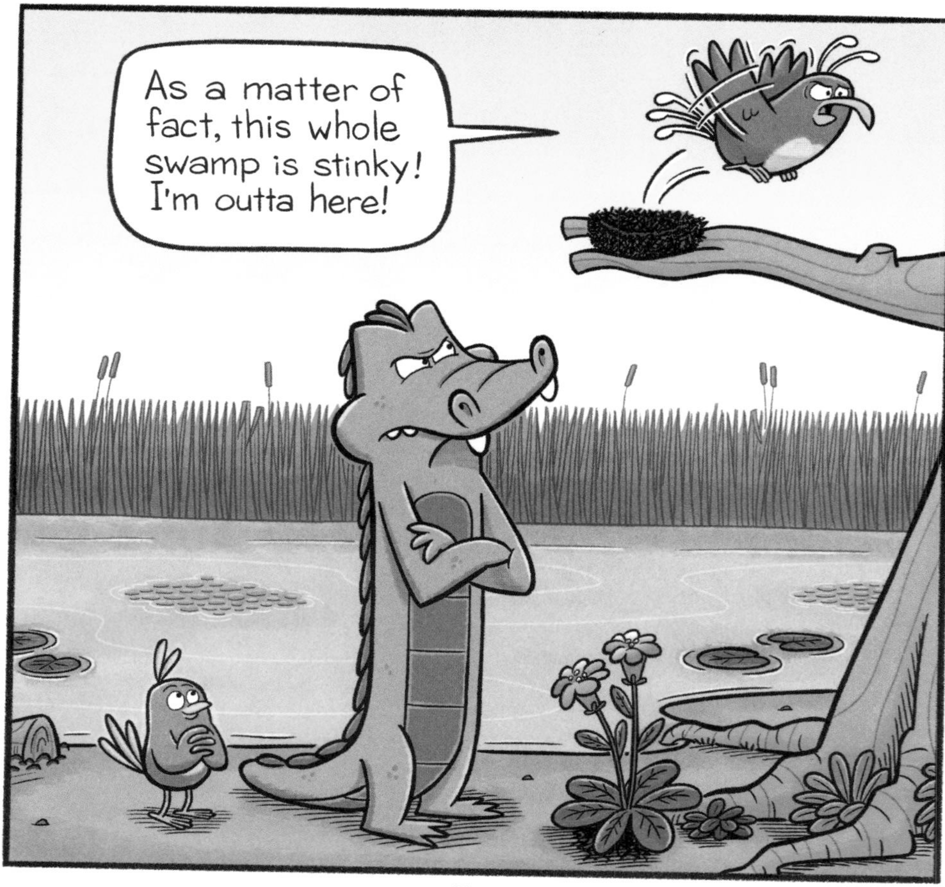
As a matter of fact, this whole swamp is stinky! I'm outta here!

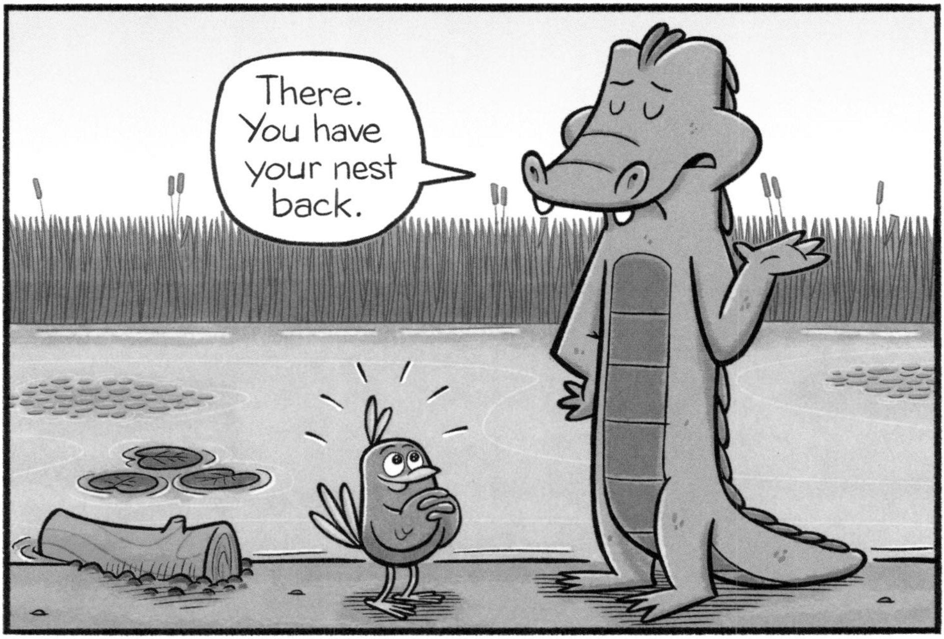
There. You have your nest back.

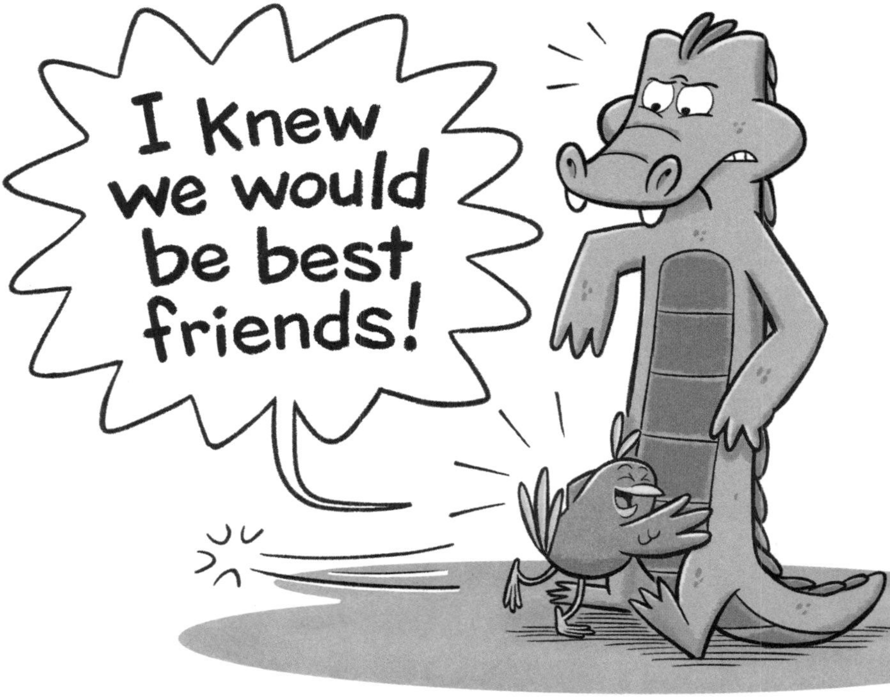
I knew we would be best friends!

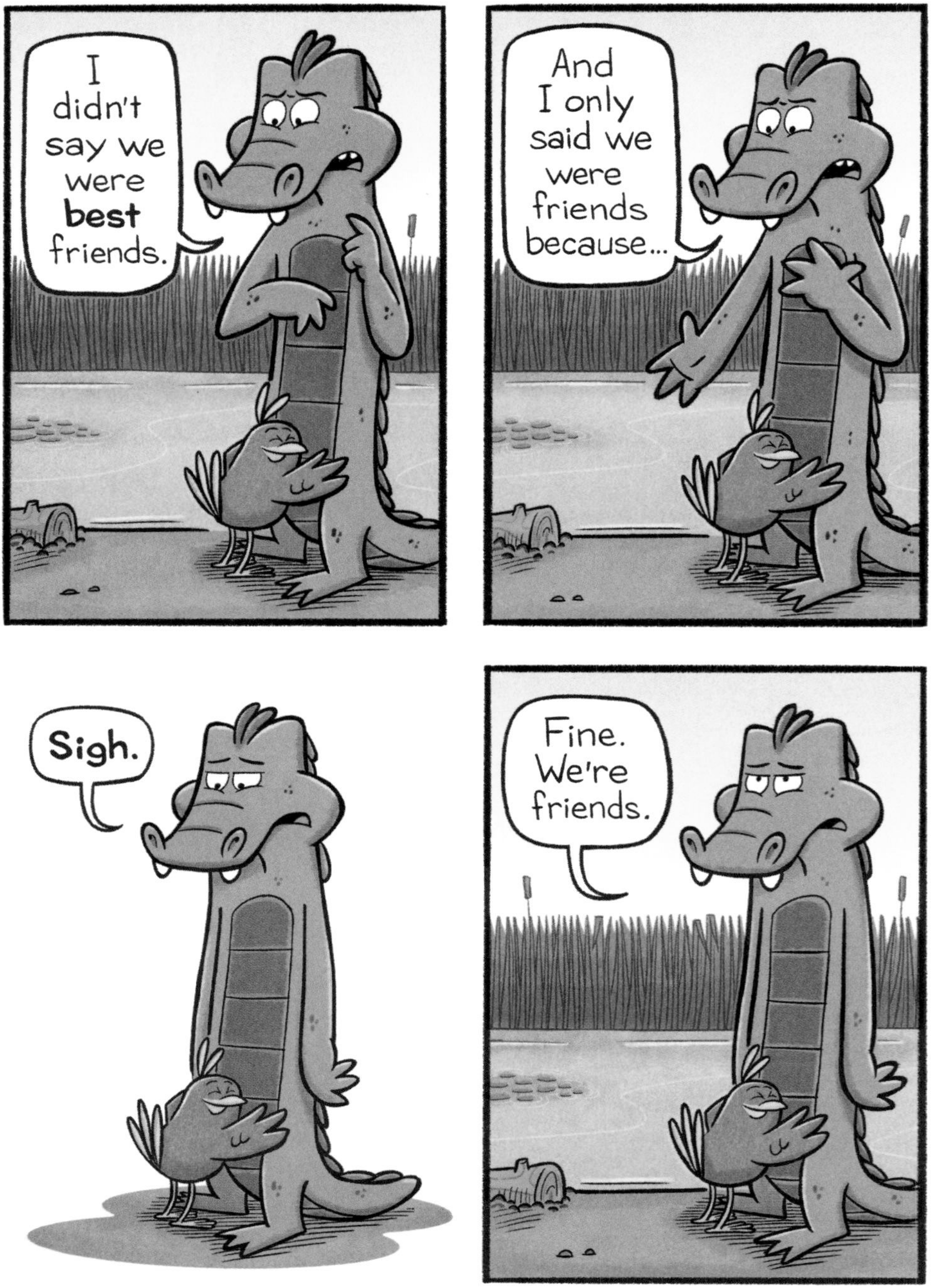
I didn't say we were **best** friends.
And I only said we were friends because...
Sigh.
Fine. We're friends.

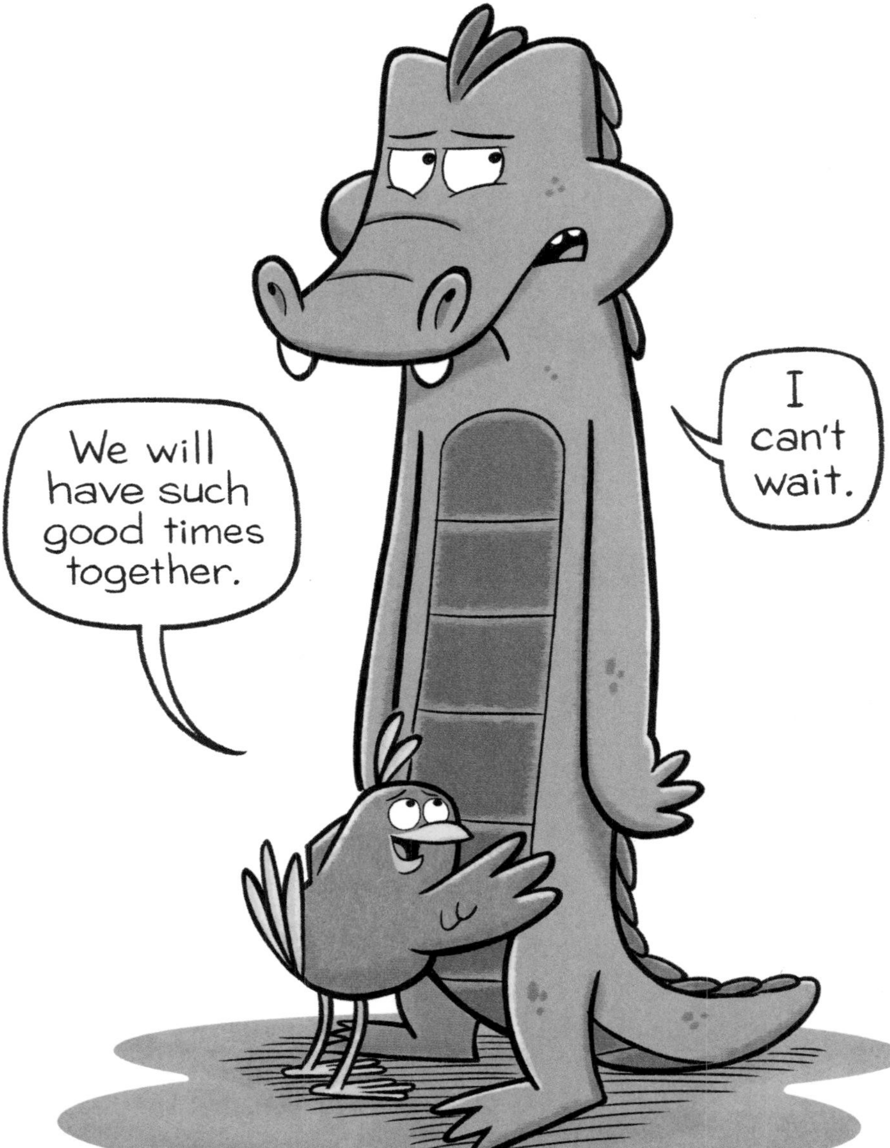
We will have such good times together.
I can't wait.

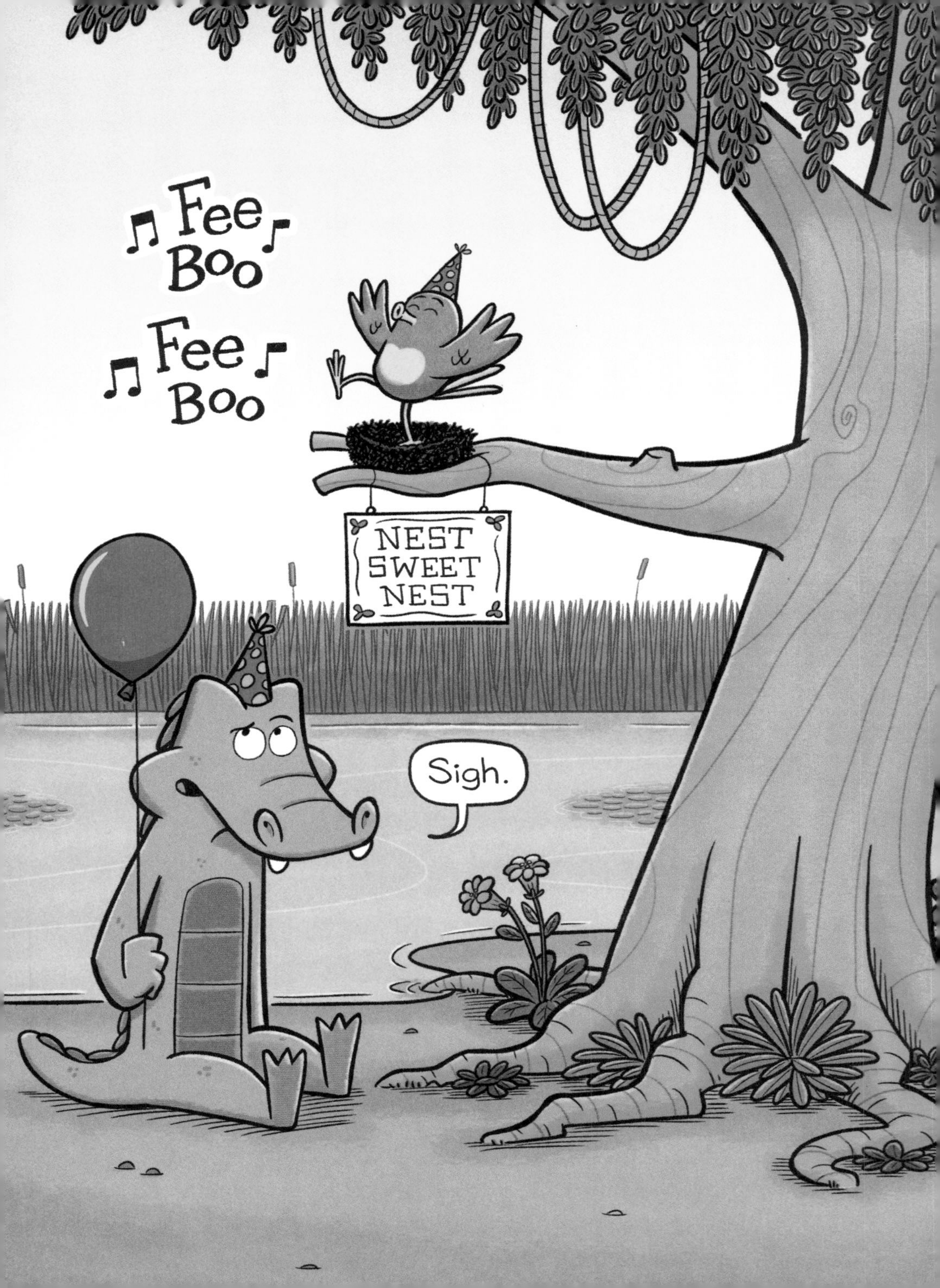
Fee Boo
Fee Boo
NEST SWEET NEST
Sigh.

HarperAlley is an imprint of HarperCollins Publishers.

Beak & Ally #1: Unlikely Friends
Copyright © 2021 by Norm Feuti
All rights reserved. Manufactured in Canada.
No part of this book may be used or reproduced in any manner whatsoever without
written permission except in the case of brief quotations embodied in critical
articles and reviews. For information address HarperCollins Children's Books, a
division of HarperCollins Publishers, 195 Broadway, New York, NY 10007.
www.harperalley.com

Library of Congress Control Number: 2020937706
ISBN 978-0-06-302157-0 (hardcover) — ISBN 978-0-06-302158-7 (pbk.)

Typography by Norm Feuti
22 23 24 25 26 TC 10 9 8 7 6 5 4 3

First Edition